VERBUM FORTIUS EST QUAM PECCATUM
CUM CULPA DIMIDIATA

STORY SYNOPSIS

Deep in the frozen heart of the Arctic, the world's most feared monster has hidden away for centuries from the prying eyes of mankind.

But now a desperate stranger has ventured to this timeless wasteland in search of the monster. Not to hunt or kill him like all other men before him.

No, this man has come seeking the monster's help.

In the darkened alleyways of Chicago, terrible experiments in bringing the dead back to life are again underway, filling the streets with soulless, undead wretches.

And the only one who can stop the dark experiments is the creature that first crossed the threshold of death all those many years ago. A creature forged from the charnel house itself, brought to life through the burning pain of electricity. Stitched together from corpses coughed from their graves.

With his new companion, the creature known as Frankenstein's Monster returns to the world of man. A world that hates and reviles him. To battle the horrifying results of his own dark legacy.

BONE WELDER

For

Donna
Dagan
Bronwyn

The torches that light my way
through the darkness.

BOOK ONE

BONE WELDER

GREG KISHBAUGH

EVILEYE

AN EVILEYE BOOK

January 2014

Published by
Pulp+Pixel Entertainment Company
301 East Congress Parkway, #1981
Crystal Lake, Illinois 60039

Editorial Director
A.N. Ommus

Cover Image: Shutterstock

Author photo by Bronwyn Kishbaugh

The *Bone Welder* logo, Evileye Books logo, and opening Latin epigraph are trademarks and service marks of Pulp+Pixel Entertainment Company.

This is a work of fiction. Similarities to persons, living, dead, undead, or otherwise out of their minds are neither intended, nor should be inferred.

Cover art direction, book and title design by Viktor Färro.

ISBN: 978-0-9848800-6-5

For more information about this series or other books published by Evileye Books, please visit Evileyebooks.com.

Produced in the United States of America.

— 6:23 —

BONE WELDER

THE MAN.

THE GREAT SHIP MADE ITS WAY toward the frozen heart of the North Pole.

From the bow of the *Nostromo*, Jonas Burke watched as its thundering steel hull shattered the patchwork puzzle of the ice, bursting and splintering it into a thousand lifeless shards that would recongeal and become one again after the ship had passed.

They had been at sea for three weeks now, and Jonas could no longer remember how it felt to have solid ground beneath his feet. The crew whiled away the lonely hours below deck drinking and gambling; Jonas preferred the silence of the deck, with only the shrill banshee clarion of the wind as his companion.

He watched the ice. Transfixed.

A place of breathtaking beauty. Nature both elegant and cruel, beautiful and vicious.

Silk-blue glaciers drifted atop steel-cold waters.

Sky and sea were one, indistinguishable from one another. Life sparse. Air brittle. The land untenable and ephemeral for it was not land at all. And at any moment it could slough off into the sea and disappear, lost to time and memory.

As Jonas looked out into the frigid eternity, his eyes weakened by the sun's constant glare, he imagined he could see the entire history of the earth written in the ice. The wars, the triumphs, the famines, the celebrations. Each generation of man in the eternal parade of history scrawled across the canvas of white.

Time, forever frozen.

And out there somewhere, hidden away in the frozen crevices, tucked into the stark blue shadows of the ice, Jonas knew there lurked a killer. A beast. And the reason Jonas Burke had journeyed to this frigid, desolate place.

To track the most maligned creature known to mankind—a beast who filled the pages of innumerable books, whose ghastly visage rampaged across countless flickering screens and haunted the dreams of young and old alike.

Jonas Burke had seen horrors blacker than any midnight. Had felt pain more searing than flame, more intense than death itself.

Now, there was nowhere else he could turn. No other option left.

No one else who could help him.

And so he traveled through waters as cold as the moon's heart to look into the eyes of a monster.

Jonas knew it was out there.

In the ice.

Waiting.

THE MONSTER.

SOMEONE WAS COMING. He could feel it. Sense it. Like a whisper carried along the Arctic winds.

He had come to this land of ice and snow and unrelenting cold to escape the eyes of man.

They had hunted and hounded him, mercilessly battered him with clubs, pitchforks and torches as if he were no better than an animal.

So he had come here. Many, many years ago.

But he knew someday they would return. He could turn his back on mankind, but he could not expect mankind to do the same.

The cold nipped at him, even through the dense coat he had fashioned from polar bear fur. He turned his head into the crying wind.

It would not be long.

He wondered if the stories they told about him remained the same. It was all a pack of lies, but men never seemed to tire of the tale.

Created from the limbs of corpses. Brought to life by a mad scientist. That much may have been true, but what about the rest?

That he had killed his creator's young brother. And then framed the maid for the horrid crime. And murdered the scientist's best friend. It was one absurdity after another. But they all chose to believe the imaginings of a nineteen-year-old girl instead of listen to the truth.

So be it.

It did not matter now.

Someday perhaps the truth would be known. Perhaps not. He could not weigh down his mind with thoughts of that now.

He must remain focused. Clear in his thinking. For the hands of man were reaching out for him again. Coming to reclaim him. He was sure of it.

And if man was seeking him yet again, it could be for no other reason than to resume the hunt. To finish what had begun so many years prior.

The air was so cold it burned.

Yes. Someone was coming.

Soon.

And he would be ready for him.

LANDFALL.

HE ARRIVED IN THE INUIT VILLAGE, weak-kneed from the long journey and ashen-faced from a withdrawn bout of seasickness. The villagers would not speak to him. They averted their eyes, shuffling past Jonas as if he were a spectre. And when he whispered the name Aningan into the frigid gray air, the villagers shuffled past even faster. Afraid.

"They think you are crazy," Jonas heard a strong voice say behind him. Captain Owen Stacey slapped him on the back. Hard.

"Is that what *you* think?"

Jonas turned, and found comfort in the captain's familiar smile. "You tell me. In eleven years as Captain of this ship, you are my first stowaway. Not many men would risk what you have for a trip to the North Pole."

Owen Stacey was a large man, thick-fisted and round as a tire. After Jonas had been discovered in one of the darkened cargo bays below decks, the captain had listened to his mad story, and while Jonas was certain he believed nothing that he said, he was at least willing to show great compassion.

"The Inuit will feed, clothe and shelter you until we return," the Captain said.

"Why?"

"Because I have asked them to. I have spent half my life up here, Jonas, and I have made friends."

"There is nothing I can say to express my gratitude. Your kindness . . ."

Jonas felt the words trail away, half-formed, a pinch of guilt forming in his gut for the gentle subterfuge he had so far engaged in. For the fact that he was no true stowaway, and that Captain Stacey would never be privy to the entire truth as to how Jonas had gotten this far.

But Jonas realized that had the *Nostromo* been helmed by a lesser man than Owen Stacey, his journey would surely have been much different. Filled with accusations and bluster and legal threats.

Instead, Captain Stacey had arranged for his safe care, and had agreed to return for him in six days when the *Nostromo* crept slowly back from gathering ice core samples farther north, deeper into the frozen heart of the world.

Jonas Burke vowed that some day he would repay this man for his kindness.

A fierce wind sprang suddenly from off the frozen ocean, raking the southeast coast of Ellesmere Island with deadly cold. The *Nostromo* had traveled north through the Nares Strait, the channel separating Ellesmere from Greenland, before ferrying Jonas across the frozen ice to the Inuit village, the northernmost human settlement on the globe. Just 800 kilometers from the North Pole, it was a desolate and unearthly land, thought Jonas. A land cut off from time and space.

The Inuit had a name for this frozen wasteland: Aujuittuq. *The place that never thaws.*

"I'm afraid this search of yours . . . ," the Captain struggled to find the right words. "I hope it doesn't lead to disappointment."

"I have no choice other than to believe he exists. I will find him or I won't. I have done all I can. Either way, I will be ready to go when you return."

"Six days is a long time out on this ice. It will seem an eternity."

"I have been through worse." Jonas extended a gloved hand. Stacey's huge hand swallowed his and they shook.

"You never answered my question," Jonas said, as the Captain walked slump-shouldered into a rising wind.

The Captain turned.

"Do you think I'm crazy?"

The Captain smiled, warm and hearty. "Good luck, Jonas," he said, before turning away again. "I hope you find what you are searching for."

Jonas stood quietly, the wind howling in his ears, watching as the sleds raced back to the *Nostromo*. A thundering crash rang out as the ship, a gleaming silver leviathan in the waning light of day, broke free from the ice's grip and journeyed northward.

To Jonas, the shattering ice brought to mind the sound of breaking bones.

FITFUL.

THE SETTLEMENT was a tightly scattered amalgam of wooden houses, perched upon stilts, elevating them above the permafrost. The homes could not be built directly upon the ground or risk the softening of the earth during the summer months swallowing the tidy buildings in small, terrifying gulps.

Despite the small homes, with generators and snowmobiles perched in the back of each, the Inuit still lived lives not much separated from those of their ancestors centuries before. They still survived entirely from the hunt—seal, polar bear, walrus, musk ox, beluga, narwhale and fish and whatever else Mother Nature would yield in this unforgiving stretch of the world. And while on the hunt, they sought shelter as their people had done for a millennia. They erected igloos.

As Jonas roused slowly from a deep and fitful sleep, he marveled at the warmth the domed ice shelter provided. A mat of caribou hides spread out beneath him, velvet soft.

Many of the permanent shelters on Ellesmere had additional rooms. Empty, warm and inviting. But none of the Inuit would open their doors for Jonas. A generous people by nature, they were nonetheless unwilling to allow this stranger into their homes. This dark-eyed man from the south who asked about Aningan.

And, so, Jonas had no other option than to settle into the igloo. And welcome the sleep that came over him. Cloaked him.

But only for a short time. Dark dreams soon tugged him awake.

He propped himself up on one elbow, and stared into the short tunnel that served as entryway to the igloo, a flap of sealskin rustling in the wind. Was he really out there, Jonas wondered? Wandering the ice, a spectre out of time?

Jonas knew that when the Inuit snuck fleeting glimpses into his haunted eyes they must surely have wondered what could have driven a man to such lengths. How could a sane man make sense of any of this? But Jonas Burke knew that rationale thought was the luxury of the content and satisfied, of the downright lucky. When life turned black, when normal day-to-day existence became a somber, morbid struggle, sane men became noticeably less stable, the ground beneath their feet crumbling to nothing more substantial than sand.

No one knew this better than Jonas Burke.

He had once been certain, like everyone else, that the Frankenstein Monster was but a figment of a teenaged girl's feverish imagination. But when Jillian became ill— grew too tired and weak to even smile when he said he loved her—he began to grasp at anything, no matter how perverse or beyond reason, to prevent himself from slipping further into a helpless despair. That is when he began to visit musty occult bookstores and frequent the darkened libraries of academia. And that is when, after pouring over arcane texts left untouched on shelves for decades, day after day, month after month, a concept began to crystallize; Mary Shelley was creative, for certain, but the tale of Frankenstein's Monster had not sprung solely from her imagination.

She had derived her tale from a true incident. A young doctor who discovered the secret of death, who welded lifeless flesh and bone into a walking, thinking being. Victor Frankenstein had found a way to cheat death, to outwit the Grim Reaper himself. He had discovered a formula for re-animating the dead.

And as Jillian's breath became shallow and stale, Jonas knew what he had to do. But Jonas Burke could never anticipate the pain his decision would bring, to himself and his beautiful daughter. And now, after all he had been through, there was only one creature on earth he could turn to, a beast believed to be a cold-blooded murderer, a brute with the strength to tear a man's still beating heart from his chest. This was his only remaining hope.

The last the Western world had heard of the Monster, it had smuggled its way onto a freighter bound for the North Pole (just as Jonas had seemingly done) and, after struggling with the anger and disillusionment of being abandoned by his creator—his father—the Monster killed Victor Frankenstein. Strangled him. And then it receded into a life of isolation amongst the ice. The Monster could not age, could not die, because it was composed of flesh that had already been buried. He was already dead. So Jonas deduced he must still be here, in the North Pole. Shuffling among the glaciers, waiting for eternity to end.

Jonas laid his head back down upon the silken softness of the caribou skins. Closed his eyes. Prayed for the sleep he knew would not return.

Instead his darkened mind filled with wavering images of his wife, his daughter. Like heat mirages. His life as it had been. Before the darkness had settled into it forever.

And then something else. A figure. Brutish, lumbering, more shadow than man, more monster than human.

Jonas had seen the term Aningan for the first time while reading the journals of a French explorer named Luc Montclaire. Montclaire had traveled to the North Pole just after the turn of the century and had written of a legend that he said consumed the Inuit people. They had festivals to honor this being. They prayed to him before the hunt and they blessed their children by his name. The legend of Aningan. *The Dead Who Walks.*

Jonas held his eyes tightly closed, as if trying to will himself to sleep. Outside the wind screamed like an ice-white demon.

In the morning, he would find someone in the Intuit village to answer his questions. If not, he would venture out on his own.

Images of the beast reeled through his mind all through the black night. Stitches holding together dead flesh. A terrible creature more dead than alive.

And in Jonas's fitful, tormented dreams, it was not he who was tracking the Monster, but the other way around. Coming for him. Shambling hump-shouldered through sheets of snow, hands outstretched, cold fingers eager to settle into the soft flesh of Jonas's neck.

AN OFFER.

IT WAS A NEARLY IMPERCEPTIBLE SHIFT in the cold that awakened him. A drop in temperature as subtle as a whisper.

The flap at the entrance of the igloo had been moved. Someone was here with him.

He could feel the man's presence before a word was spoken.

"This creature you seek, what is it you want from it?" The man's voice was deep and sonorous, resonating like a stone kicked down a well.

Jonas sat up, his vision blurred from sleep. An Inuit man crouched on his haunches before him, his brown skin spider-webbed with wrinkles, his hands gnarled as tree roots. His tiny black eyes sparkled, two obsidian jewels.

"I seek his help," Jonas said.

"From a monster? What help can it possibly offer?"

Jonas leaned forward. "Then you know of him. Aningan?"

"Every Inuit for the past two centuries knows of the Dead Who Walks. What you are planning . . . it is madness. You should not do this thing. Go home. Back to your family."

"I don't have one," Jonas said, as cold as the surrounding ice.

"You do not want to see Aningan. No man wants to see that."

"Is he that terrible? That frightening?"

Jonas stared into the weather-lashed face of the Inuit, into the black marble abyss of his eyes. "The stench of the grave surrounds him," he said. "The pall of death. I plead with you to leave now."

"And go where?" Jonas said. "I have traveled to the end of the world to find him. Risked everything."

"I can see your suffering," the man said. "It rises from you. Swims in the darkness of your eyes. But do not think you can suffer no more. Do not think that much greater pain can never reach you. If you do this thing, I fear you will discover an entirely new level of despair. One you could never have imagined."

"There are times a man simply feels there is nothing else left to lose."

"That's what I am telling you," said the man. "There is *always* something left to lose. But I'm afraid you won't know that until it is gone."

Jonas clapped his gloved hands together, rubbed them, warmth spreading slowly to his fingers. "I have not come here for understanding. Or for sympathy."

"Why have you come?"

Jonas considered the question, turned it over in his mind. Truth was, he was not altogether certain he knew the answer himself. "For another chance."

The old man sighed, a hummingbird rush of air. "You are a fool." He turned and trundled toward the igloo's domed entrance. To Jonas the man now seemed so small and frail.

The old man paused, then over his shoulder, said. "We will leave at first light. I will show you the way. I do not want you stumbling out there on the ice, lost, confused."

"Why do you care?"

"About you? I don't. I care about my people. And I'm afraid that your ignorance and arrogance will anger Aningan. And that you may even be fool enough to lead him back here. I will not have that. So I will take you as far as common sense will allow. Make sure that your intrusion here no longer poses a threat to us. Then you will be on your own."

"And then . . .? If I find him, what do you think he will do?"

The Inuit slipped through the sealskin flap that separated the igloo from a night as cold as the Reaper's blade. Without turning around the old man said, "He will kill you."

BLINDING WHITE.

JONAS BURKE SHOOK THE BUILDUP of ice crystals from his gloves and trudged forward. The old man, Anauk, was hunched into the clawing wind, bent beneath the weight of his carryall.

To all outward appearances, Jonas looked very much like the Inuit from the settlement he had just left behind. Upper body swallowed by an enormous coat stitched together from caribou, his hands, feet and legs tucked snugly into sealskin. The only nod to the twenty-first century was a pair of polarized snow goggles that protected his eyes from the infinite blanket of shimmering ice.

"Not much further," Anauk shouted, his voice trailing away in the wind.

They had set out from the Inuit village a little more than four hours earlier, when the sun had just peeked out over the icy lip of the world. The sunrise was the most beautiful Jonas had ever seen. Burning bright in the eastern sky like a rocket's afterburner. But it had dissipated quickly. A gray pall quickly settled over the sky, the sun's bright light quickly obscured behind a veil of blowing snow and ice.

The torrential gusts were like a thunderstorm of needles against the exposed areas of Jonas's face. His cheeks were now raw and brittle. "Surely, nothing will be out on a day like this," Jonas shouted to his guide.

"What concern is snow and wind to the dead," Anauk shouted. "Aningan will be out. If not, I can show you to his lair. Either way, you will get what you came for."

Jonas, following the blurred outline of Anauk, pressed forward. The elements seemed to converge into one monstrous, malicious being. Under three layers of clothing Jonas's body still felt vulnerable and exposed. In the distance, jagged blue mountains of ice lined the horizon like witches' teeth.

They leaned into the biting wind, struggling with every step, hour after hour. Nothingness stretched before them to all four corners of the world. It was like walking in a void. Jonas kept his eyes cast downward, watching the tips of his boots as they trudged through the snow.

"How much further?" he screamed.

Anauk stopped, pointed into the distance. "There is a rise in the ice up ahead. You will find him there. At the base of the glacier. Not far."

Jonas squinted. A dark stain interrupted the perfect virgin white landscape. "What is it?"

"Underground ice caves," said Anauk. "They wind mile after mile below us, like sleeping serpents. A man could spend a lifetime trying to find his way back out." Anauk stood motionless for a moment as the wind buffeted him with fine crystals of snow, whitening the fur collar rimming his face. Then he quietly turned and trudged in the opposite direction, the wind now at his back, doubling back over the footprints he had left in the snow.

"Wait a minute. Where are you going?" Jonas said.

"I told you I would not face him with you. This is where we part ways. I have taken you as far as I can."

"What if he is not there? How will I get back?"

"He will be there."

Jonas called out to the old man, shouting to be heard above the roar of the wind. "Do you fear him that much?"

Anauk smiled, wrinkles webbing in the corners of his eyes. "Don't you?" He turned from Jonas and shuffled back toward the Inuit village, toward safety. Toward home.

Despite Anuak's repeated warnings that he would not accompany Jonas to the end of his journey, being left alone in complete frozen desolation still came as a shock. There were a thousand different ways for a solitary man to die out here, Jonas knew, and he suddenly felt a sense of isolation he had never before experienced. It was like the entire world had been swept away, leaving him foundering in an endless sea of white.

As the shrill Arctic air howled around him, he stared at the black abyss Anauk had pointed out to him, the yawning hole in the earth where a monster dwelled.

Aningan's lair.

Jonas started forward again, hesitantly. There was nothing else he could do. Even if he were never to return, if the brute that awaited him in the ice cave snapped his neck, he had no other option. Jillian had no other hope.

He lowered his gaze, back to the tips of his boots as Anauk had advised, shuffling, shuffling, the snow swirling around each step.

As Jonas drew closer, the black hole lost its sharpness; clearly defined from a distance, it was now becoming increasingly difficult to see. After a few minutes, a blank white slate stretched before him. The cave entrance was nowhere to be seen, like it had been washed away. Vanished. Jonas stopped in his tracks, panic seizing him.

Surrounded by a never-ending canvas of ice and snow, and unable to locate the underground caves, rivulets of fear trickled through him. He turned slowly, surveying the landscape. Through the blurring haze of snow he could see a slump-shouldered figure shuffling along the ice. Anauk.

Jonas sighed. All was not lost. All he need do was reverse direction, catch up with his guide and admit the folly of his adventure.

But . . . strangely, it appeared that Anauk was moving *toward* him, instead of away. And the blurred figure was advancing at a much greater speed than the old Inuit would surely have been able to muster.

Faster and faster. Bearing down on him.

By the time Jonas was able to separate the lumbering form from the cascading snow, it was already too late. The polar bear barreled down upon him, teeth bared, its fur bristling.

Jonas's first hardwired instinct, however hopeless, was to flee.

He turned. Tried to run in a loping shuffle, the caribou fur weighing him down, mooring him. Where were the caves? Where?! If he could reach the entrance before the bear crashed down upon him . . .

His feet felt anchored in stone, the snow suddenly leaden. As the ceaseless expanse of snow deadened his vision, Jonas gave into the futility of outrunning the beast. He turned back toward the charging animal and waited for the great muscled weight of the white bear to crash down upon him.

Through the driving snow, the bear rumbled toward him. Closer. And closer still. Until Jonas could nearly feel the heat coming from its foamed muzzle.

But then . . . another figure. Emerging from the curtain of snow, moving with an intensity that rivaled that of the bear. Cloaked in fur, Jonas thought it was perhaps another bear, maybe even his attacker's mate. But, no, this animal moved on only two legs.

A man.

He yelled out to the bear, drawing its attention away from Jonas. Even in the haze of snow, Jonas could see it was a large man, shoulders round and muscled, legs thick. He was covered head to toe in various furs, a patchwork of tattered pelts, the most prominent of which was white.

The polar bear, lips curled away from yellowing fangs, turned its attention away from Jonas and toward this new intruder. And then the snow-white bear, a machine of death and destruction, its fangs flashing like daggers, its claws curving like blackened scimitars, crashed into the man, driving him to the ground, rolling its great weight over him, snarling, gnashing, consumed with rage.

Plumes of snow erupted as man and beast thrashed on the ground, obscuring Jonas's vision even further. He could catch nothing beyond short, staccato glimpses. A flash of the bear's snarling muzzle. A flash of the man's gloved hands around the bear's neck.

And then . . . a horrible, wrenching cry. Deep and guttural.

A sudden splash of warmth spread over Jonas's cheek. He wiped his seal-skinned glove over his rawboned cheek; it came away red with blood.

At Jonas's feet the snow was splattered crimson, pools of blood seeping into the snow, fading to pink.

From the driving curtain of snow, a hulking figure emerged. Head bent low, the wind beating at his back. Rivulets of blood bloomed up both arms, staining the fur of his coat and gloves.

His face was hidden behind a cowl of caribou skin. Jonas could see nothing more than the man's mouth, lips peeled away in a grimace. Skeletal teeth.

When the man spoke his voice was as thick as the dirt of the grave.

"Why have you come seeking me?"

UNDERGROUND.

JONAS'S EYES OPENED UPON A SMALL FIRE, popping sharply as it devoured a lump of seal blubber sitting on the ice. A polar bear fur lay sprawled out beneath him, whisper soft. He rubbed his temples and sat up. He tried to remember falling asleep put couldn't piece together exactly what had happened. His head throbbed.

"Not many men have been foolish enough to follow me here. To track me down like some animal," a voice said.

Jonas turned.

He was surrounded by ice. On all sides. As if he were entombed.

He sat in a small alcove, carved from the ice itself. He knew immediately what it was: A lair. He could feel the enormity of the ice above him pressing down, a thundering weight. Jonas wondered just how far below the surface he had been carried.

In the corner of the alcove, perched upon a throne-like edifice that had been carved directly into the ice, was the man he had seen coming toward him through the fury of the snow. The man who had killed a polar bear with his bare hands.

But more than just a man. Jonas was well aware of that. A Monster. A creature brought forth from the dead, stitched together from corpses. A thing forged from the charnel house itself.

The crackling fire was the only light, projecting distorted shadows along the walls and ceiling.

The Monster sat rigidly, completely cloaked in a long, flowing polar bear fur. Like the cowl he had worn out on the ice, the coat was hooded and the Beast's face was obscured in shadow.

"But you are not the first," he said.

"Others have sought me, as well."

Jonas's mouth went dry. "I did not mean to disturb you."

"Yet you have."

The Monster remained stoic, unflinching. As if he too were carved from the ice.

The Monster's hands, now ungloved, protruded from beneath the white fur. Jonas immediately noticed the difference and struggled not to stare. The Monster's left hand was much as he would have expected—discolored a pasty yellow-white, like curdled milk, with scars crisscrossing the bridge of the knuckles.

But the right hand . . . it was noticeably smaller, almost delicate in its features. Where the left hand was meaty and cumbersome, the right hand was smooth and porcelain.

The Monster raised the left hand like a mallet and slammed it down upon his makeshift throne. "Tell me why you have come here."

Jonas stood, his temples throbbing, his throat raw as a wound. "You are really him? Is it possible?"

The Monster sighed. "If you know anything about me at all, you are aware that patience is not one of my virtues."

"Most of the world believes you to be fiction," Jonas said.

"But you knew better, eh? What made you a believer?"

"I have seen the possibilities of reanimation."

The Monster leaned forward. "You what?"

"I know it's possible."

"You are a liar. And a fool."

"I tell you the truth. I have seen the dead brought back to life."

"You have seen no such thing. The dead never return to life. They may be reanimated; they may be reconstituted, stitched together with the stinking remains of other bodies, but they can never *live*."

"In Chicago, there is a man . . . a man who knows Victor Frankenstein's secrets. He's even . . ."

"He has even what?"

"He's expanded upon them."

The fingers of the left hand, thick and stiff as shotgun shells, began to drum against the ice. "What does that mean?"

"No longer must pieces of various corpses be used, stitched together, as you say. Entire bodies can be reanimated."

The Monster laughed. "How do you know all this?"

"I used to work for him. I know all about his . . . experiments."

"And you have come here to regale me with his scientific advances?"

"No," Jonas said quietly, staring into the cold gray eyes of the Monster. Eyes like hardened steel. "I have come to ask for your help."

"My help?" The Monster roared incredulously.

"I want to stop him. To put an end to what he is doing."

"And why should I help you stop this man?"

"His name is Lucias Angel . . . he was created, as were you, in 1806 by the same man who gave you life. Dr. Victor Frankenstein. Only he was not hammered together with the broken pieces of dead bodies. He was reanimated. Brought back from death. Whole and complete."

The Monster tilted his head back, the cowl falling away. Jonas could now clearly see the lifeless white pupils, the squalid skin stretched tight over high cheekbones.

"And this is why you came here? To tell me Victor Frankenstein created another? That I am not the only one?"

"Think about what it means," Jonas urged.

"It means my father continues to bring me pain and grief two centuries after his death."

"It means . . ." Jonas said, "That you are not entirely alone."

"This Angel is nothing to me."

"Yes, he is," Jonas replied. "He is your brother."

BELLY OF THE BEAST.

DESPITE BEING SURROUNDED BY FIRE, Jonas Burke shivered. In the bowels of the North Pole, curled up on the yellow-white softness of a polar bear fur, there was no escaping the all-consuming coldness. The lifeless air. He rubbed his hands in front of the fire, but there was nothing. Like kissing someone you had fallen out of love with, it just left him empty inside.

He thought of Jillian, of her warm breath as she lay sleeping on his chest when she was a baby. Of her milk-pure smile and the giggle that shook her whole body. The more his thoughts turned to her the colder he grew.

Cold and shivering.

The Monster had not spoken a word since Jonas had told him of Lucias Angel. He leaned forward and buried his shattered face in his hands.

To Jonas he looked simply like . . . a man.

There were no bolts in his neck and his skin was not green. The top of his head was round, not flat, and although a wide, ragged scar ran across his forehead and down his left cheek, there were no others on his face. He was big, but not much taller than Jonas. Maybe six feet, four inches, Jonas guessed. No more.

His eyes were sad, drained of color and half-lidded. His teeth were straight but stained brown. His skin was a sickly, sunless white, like the flesh of a chicken after its feathers had been plucked. He certainly would have turned heads, may have even frightened some people a great deal, but he was no monster.

Monsters are malicious, without remorse, tearing at their victims with glee. A man like Lucias Angel fit that description better than the pathetic wretch before Jonas now.

He was too consumed by sadness, too shriveled with shame to be a Monster.

"What should I call you?" Jonas asked.

"My name is Victor. Like my father."

They had moved from the small confines of the room in which Jonas regained consciousness to an enormous, cavernous room where Victor apparently passed most of his lonely hours. The silk-blue ceiling of ice stretched far overhead and the room itself was so large that its furthest reaches were obscured in shadow. In each of its four corners, seal blubber fires popped and shimmered. Another fire, larger than the other four combined, roared in the center of the room. It was over this fire that Jonas vainly attempted to warm himself.

The floor was scattered with polar bear rugs, three and four deep in some places, and next to a bulging pile of furs—which Victor obviously used as a bed—there was a seemingly endless ocean of books. Shakespeare, Milton, Dante, Lawrence. Some modern masters, as well. Vonnegut, Ellison and Bradbury. The books were dog-eared, the covers scuffed and worn. *Hamlet*, *The Grapes of Wrath*, *Fahrenheit 451*, *Slaughterhouse Five*, *Great Expectations*. A complete set of encyclopedia. An atlas that looked as if it predated the first world war.

"They are my only companions," Victor offered solemnly.

"I used to love to read. Many years ago."

"And now you do not?"

Jonas shrugged. "I would read to my daughter every night. When she was young and then . . ." Jonas let the sentence trail away like a soft breeze. "I wanted her to love the written word as I did."

Victor lowered himself to the ground, onto a mound of white fur. He sat awkwardly, one leg jutting straight out, the other tucked beneath him, his back hunched slightly.

Jonas moved away from the fire and began to pace. Maybe the movement will bring some warmth, he thought. He pulled his gloves back on and slapped them together as he walked. A black leather-bound book with a gold inscribed spine caught his eye. He bent to pick it up, then stopped himself. He glanced up at Victor. "Go ahead," he said, permissively.

Jonas lifted it from the ice, and turned it toward the firelight. He smiled.

Frankenstein, or the Modern Prometheus, by Mary Wolstonecraft Shelley.

"I loved this book when I was a boy. The movies, too." Jonas was about to say more. To tell Victor about the first time he had seen *Frankenstein*, the old, creaky black-and-white version with Boris Karloff as the doomed Monster. He and three of his friends had snuck into the Victory Theater when they were in elementary school and had been frightened nearly to death by the movie. And the hulking, dimwitted, murderous brute that was Frankenstein's Monster. But Jonas kept silent, and he knew immediately that Victor could sense his discomfort.

"I know of the films. A lumbering beast with bolts in its neck and the brain of an infant." Victor shook his head, and Jonas could see the dark pain lurking in his eyes. "That is how the world sees me. A fool."

"The world believes you to be a work of fiction." Jonas pointed to one of the tumbling stack of novels on the floor. "Just like one of your books."

"Every work of fiction has truth as its foundation."

Jonas put Shelley's classic book back where he had found it and retrieved another. *War of the Worlds*. And another. *Hard Times*. And another. *The Odyssey*.

"How many times have you read these?" Jonas asked.

"Far too many to count."

"What is your favorite?"

"That is like asking to name a favorite child."

"How do you get them?"

"The Inuit. They bring them to me. They leave them as peace offerings so I will not hurt them."

Jonas lifted his eyes from a copy of *The Martian Chronicles*, its spine cracked and brittle. "And would you?"

"Would I what?"

"Would you hurt them if they didn't?"

Victor smiled, his pallid skin almost translucent in the dim light of the rooms' five fires. "Maybe you have read *too* much, Jonas. I'm afraid that young Miss Shelley did not get all her facts straight. But if your question is, Did I kill those people, as described in the book . . . my father's young brother and the maid . . . and Elizabeth? No, I killed no one." He sat silent for a moment. "And I did not kill my father."

"What happened?"

Victor shook his head. "No," he said, a swelling agitation setting his eyes aflame. "You did not travel all this way to hear my story. No one cares. They have made up their own lies about me, have painted me as a bumbling brute, barely able to form a sentence. No. There is nothing left to say about me. It is *your* story that interests me. You have come here to ask for my help, and yet you have told me nothing. Why are you here, Jonas Burke? What compelled you to cross the ends of the earth to look for me?"

"I told you. Your brother . . ."

"Don't lie to me. He is a smoke screen. Tell me the real reason you are here."

Jonas felt a sharp pinprick of pain in his heart. An electric charge of longing and rage. Whenever he thought of Jillian the reaction was the same. Horror. Shame. Denial.

He had never told anyone the truth. Not in its entirety. How could he? What he had done was beyond belief, beyond the reasoning of any rational man.

But now the truth must come out—the whole truth. He had come all this way. He owed it to her.

"I had a daughter. A beautiful girl." Jonas spoke haltingly, tears welling in his eyes. "She was taken from me. She was only eighteen." The tears burned. "Eighteen. Sweet God." He was crying now, gently, trying to be discreet. But failing. "So young. And she was all I had." Jonas paused, trying to catch his breath, to calm himself. He looked up at Victor who now stood before him, his eyes pulled into a question mark, his mouth drawn into a razor-thin line. He was shaking.

"Jonas. What did you do?"

"She was so young," Jonas repeated. He wanted to tell the story, everything that had happened, everything he had been through, but he could not find the words. The utter degradation—the despair—was too much to bear. He had sold his baby's soul into eternal damnation. He had spit in God's eye.

Victor grabbed him by the arms and shook him. Hard. "Jonas, what did you do?"

"Lucias, your brother . . . he said he could help. He said he could bring my little girl back."

Victor's grip slackened and his hands fell to his side. "Oh no. You didn't."

"I missed her so much. I couldn't go on . . . couldn't live without her. He said he could bring her back to me. He said that she was too young, there was no reason for her to be dead."

Victor turned away from Jonas and bowed his head to the ice.

Jonas buried his face in his hands. "I just wanted my little girl back, that's all. I wanted my precious baby to come back to me."

JONAS'S JOURNEY.

IT WAS A CRISP FALL EVENING, approaching the razor-edge of midnight, when Jillian was cut screaming from her mother's belly, four days before her expected due date. She arrived at 11:53 p.m., October 14th.

Exactly three minutes after her mother died.

Complications had set in almost immediately after arriving at the hospital, but the doctors assured Jonas there was no need for alarm. Hold her hand, they advised. Help with her breathing. Keep her calm. But at just past 11:45 the heart monitors, which for the past five hours had soothed Jonas with their steady hummingbird rhythm, began suddenly to scream. The red lines ceased spiking up and down, and instead went flat. A dull, constant beep droned from the machine like a fly caught under a glass.

"What's happening?" Jonas screamed.

No one answered him. Two doctors and a nurse rushed into the room and within seconds had ushered him out into the hallway. Twenty minutes later, one of the doctors, fresh-faced and not long out of med school, told him of the death of his wife and the birth of his daughter, all in one rambling sentence.

Years later, the pain of Katherine's death still searing his heart like a hot poker, all that he would allow his memory to call up from that night was holding his daughter for the first time. Staring into the starlight blue of her eyes and promising to devote his life to her happiness. He wanted her to struggle as little as possible with the pain of a motherless childhood; he did all he could to compensate.

Jonas had been a successful architect for a number of years already, working in the scurrying-ant bustle of Chicago's Loop; he had been heavily recruited out of Cornell, widely considered the nation's top architectural undergraduate program, and had enjoyed a high five-figure salary from the moment he received his diploma. Over the past several years he had even dipped his toe into six-figure territory with the addition of performance bonuses.

He was steeped in all the various disciplines, with a decided natural talent for neoclassicism and post-modernism but his personal taste leaned heavily toward the brooding, ornate complexities of the Gothic style.

When Jillian was born (and Katherine slipped so suddenly away) he immediately set about rearranging his schedule. No one at his agency minded; they valued Jonas too much. So the eight or nine o'clock nights that he and Katherine had grown accustomed to quickly became six o'clock. And the weekend afternoons spent behind his drawing table segued into days in the park with Jillian followed by the two of them sharing an ice cream cone; or skipping stones; or visiting the petting zoo; or just laying on a grassy knoll, with their eyes toward the heavens, watching the clouds scuffle lazily by.

Jonas experienced a great many moments of happiness in those early years, but they were bittersweet. With Jillian's first step, her first word, her first day in school, his thoughts inevitably turned to Katherine and how much she would have cherished these times. No matter how deep his love for his daughter, he could never fully put aside the anger of having lost his wife. A woman he had fallen in love with during senior year in high school and who had been his companion ever since. The incredible pain. A pinprick in the soul that continues to tear and grow. Part of the pain comes with the recognition that nothing can ever repair that hole. As long as he lived he would have to deal with the emptiness within him, as hollow and cold as a tomb.

But he had Jillian. And that got Jonas through.

She was a tremendous student, pulling straight A's through all of elementary school, and making the Dean's list in junior high school with a strong affinity for history. In high school she became involved in sports, soccer and volleyball and, for conditioning, cross-country. As early as her sophomore year there was talk of scholarships. A few colleges had already shown interest in her, both academically and athletically. She looked very much like Katherine; she had her deep, shining smile. And her intelligence and humor. She filled Jonas with a sense of pride he had never before known. Every one of her perfect smiles made him feel complete.

Then the coughing began.

It was not a concern at first. They thought it to be a cold. She stayed home from school a few days and was back on her feet. Then the coughing deepened, became more persistent. Her lungs began to rattle like she had swallowed broken glass. The doctor said it was probably bronchitis. Nothing to worry about. The doctor was an old man, pickled with age, but with a sweet face. Jonas believed him.

Then Jillian started coughing up blood. He rushed her to the emergency room. More tests were run. This time there was no sweet-faced old doctor. Nor was there anyone to advise him not to worry.

As it turned out the coughing was but a symptom of a larger problem, a consequence of a compromised immune system. The final prognosis felt to Jonas like the Devil had taken him by the hand and whispered in his ear.

Leukemia.

The prognosis doubled Jonas over. Like he had been hit in the stomach with a shovel.

Because of the acute nature of the disease, Jillian's doctors were aggressive. Chemotherapy was instituted immediately. Jillian endured the cramping, bruising, and nausea with a thin smile. It wasn't until her hair became fine and started to drift away from her scalp in clumps that the smile became more strained.

Despite the treatments, Jillian became increasingly more ill. Anemic. Fallow-eyed. Her skin nearly translucent.

The only solution, said the dour-faced doctors, was a bone marrow transplant. It would aid in allowing the chemotherapy to gain effectiveness, they told Jonas. Even so, the prognosis did not look good. Jonas watched the doctors as if through a rain-streaked window. They wavered before him like heat mirages. It was all so otherworldly and surreal.

What they were saying was this: we'll do everything we can but there is a strong chance that your little girl—the only light left in your life—is going to die.

The next morning, foggy and disoriented from lack of sleep, he arose to the buzzing of his phone on the nightstand. The voice on the other end was barely audible. Thick and syrupy, barely rising above that of a whisper.

But the caller's message was clear. Jonas was being offered a job. With a substantial raise. And full medical benefits to help with Jillian's expenses. At one of the largest, most powerful companies in the world, Arch Angel Enterprises. A company with its fingers in a thousand different markets, from assembling planes for the U.S. military to delivering heat shields for NASA's space program.

We've had our eye on you a long time, the voice said, seductive and smooth. You're being called up to the big leagues.

It was, as they say, an offer too good to refuse. Jonas never once asked why they wanted him. What he had done to so warrant such an offer. Truth was, he didn't care. It would allow him to spend more time with Jillian and to care for her more comfortably.

He had only one request.

"I want to work at night. All night. Days free."

Done, said the voice on the line. Followed by nothing but static.

And so a neighbor he had befriended—an old widower named Gus Sandson—agreed to spend the evenings at Jonas's house, attending to Jillian's needs should there be any, and Jonas began his job at Arch Angel Enterprises. It was not far from his architectural firm, just across the Chicago River, in a building that was one of the most beloved—and reviled—in the entire city. A building that had gained so much notoriety that Jonas had studied its elaborate and unorthodox architecture while attending Cornell. Much of the shuffling hordes in Chicago's loop hated its enormous stone archway. And the stained glass on the upper levels. And the flying buttress designs that had been appropriated almost stone for stone from the Bath Abbey in Bath, England. Even the glum (Jonas would say glorious) gargoyles that squatted sentry at all four points of the building's roof brought scorn from many.

Jonas, naturally, had loved the building his entire life.

Despite being in a near constant state of exhaustion, Jonas never complained. Never wavered in his commitment to spend every waking hour supporting

Jillian. Arch Angel Enterprises was expanding into markets across the globe and, as such, Jonas hit the ground running, helping to design buildings from Sao Paulo to Kuala Lumpur. He worked feverishly throughout the night, and when he arrived back home at eight a.m., the sun still just a whisper in the sky, he would brew himself a pot of coffee and prepare himself for a full day with Jillian. He survived on catnaps and caffeine.

This continued for more than two months, each day very much like the day before. Jillian's health remained in a sort of stasis, not getting better to be certain, but not deteriorating, either. That all changed on a blustery fall day, less than a week before Jillian's 18th birthday.

That's when Jonas met Cooper Shaye.

Jonas was running late.

He normally arrived outside the Arch Angel building between ten and ten fifteen in the evening, but tonight his train had broken down outside Northbrook, sitting idly on the tracks for more than twenty-five minutes.

Truth was, Jonas had nothing to fear for his tardiness. Certainly no repercussions. All his immediate supervisors worked during the day, and as long as he got his work done, they provided him a great deal of latitude.

But he hated being late, even if he was the only one who noticed.

And so he huffed along the North bank of the Chicago River, just past the 90-degree bend that shot its churning dark water into the frigid heart of Lake Michigan. The air was touched with the acrid scent of a bitter winter approaching. As if Jonas could sense the freezing winds and snow that were gathering forces, ready to descend upon the city.

He lifted his head, the cool air like a caress.

The electric yellow haze of the city's lights set the horizon ablaze like a thousand fireflies were strung up in the autumn sky, a slivered moon played hide and seek among the clouds. Jonas's thoughts turned to Jillian, lying in her bed, covered in a slick coat of sweat, a forced smile on her face as the cancer ate her away. Jonas had bent to kiss her before leaving for work and her forehead had been cool, as if her blood had run dry. He brushed a tangle of blonde hair away from her cheek and crept from her room.

Jonas checked his watch. 10:32. He turned the corner and walked toward the rear of the building. Toward the after-hours entrance. A stone archway, a much smaller replica of the one at the building's main entrance, yawned before him, a metal riveted set of double doors distracting from the Gothic design.

A wire-enmeshed light above the archway cast a wan yellow circle of radiance. Just outside the pool of light a shadow moved. Shifted. Jonas thought he heard a sigh.

"You the one with the sick girl?"

Jonas jumped. "Jesus Christ." He straightened the collar of his coat and tried to compose himself. "Who's there?' he asked into the shadows. From behind an empty dumpster a man emerged. Tall and thin and as frail as a porcelain doll, the man coughed and motioned Jonas toward him. "You're him, right?"

"What do you want?"

"You're him. With the little girl."

"How do you know me?"

The man motioned for him again. "Come over here. Out of the light."

Jonas stared toward the man, quickly darting his eyes left and right, trying to discern if anyone else was with him.

"Come on. I'm no threat to you. Just want to talk."

The man had a blue cap pulled tight over his ears. An oversized raincoat, its belt torn from the loops and dragging on the ground, hung awkwardly from his sharply angled shoulders. It hung open and Jonas could see that the man wore several layers of clothing underneath. The outermost were a pair of green pants that barely hung past his calves and a Disney World sweatshirt that had apparently been white at one time but was now a dull gray.

There were scores of homeless people in this area, and Jonas had seen them every day on his way to and from work, but this man was different. There was something about him that made Jonas go cold inside. His eyes were blue-green, muted, like watercolors mixed together. And his skin. It was pasty white, ashen. It hung from his bones like cloth. He looked sickly and feeble, and once Jonas felt comfortable with the fact that the man was alone, he decided that he was indeed not much of a threat. He stepped away from the light and into the shadows. "You haven't answered my question. How do you know me?"

"I know everybody inside this building. At least I try to."

"Why?"

The man coughed. "There's enough of us out here. Don't want any more. You met your boss yet?"

"Which one? Company has more middle managers than the Pentagon."

"Not those drones. I'm talking about the boss. *Angel*."

Jonas did not answer.

"You haven't met him yet. I can see it in your eyes. Hasn't talked to you about your girl. What's her name? Jillian. Is that right?"

As the man spoke, his cap slowly crept higher on his forehead, and Jonas could see that he wore it not so much to keep out the cold as he did to hide the thick pink scar that sloped from his right ear up into his hairline. "Who are you?" Jonas asked. "What do you want?"

"He'll come to you. He'll make promises."

"What would Lucias Angel want with me? He's one of the wealthiest, most powerful men in the world. He's had more dinners at the White House than the first lady."

The man shuffled forward, his back hunched. "He'll tell you things that seem impossible. As if your prayers have been answered. Don't be tempted. It is all a lie."

"I don't know what you're talking about."

"You will. And when he comes to you, you tell that man to go straight to hell. And you can tell him that Cooper Shaye is waiting for him. We're *all* waiting for him down here."

The man turned and disappeared into the shadows, fading away is if he were but a memory. Jonas stood for a moment, wondering how a man such as Lucias Angel would ever come to know about Jillian and, even if he did, what he could possibly offer him.

Three days passed.

Jillian's forehead grew colder and damper. Her breathing became forced, like she was trying to draw air through a straw. A full-time nurse was hired and his daughter's teenage room (with posters of rock bands still on the walls) turned quietly into a hospice. It wouldn't be long, and the reality of that sent Jonas into a spiral of hatred and depression and pain. His heart burned like it had turned rotten and begun to decay. At night he would pray, but his prayers became bitter and hateful. They changed from "Please, help my daughter," to "How could you do this to my girl?" Soon the prayers trailed away, leaving behind nothing but despair. And blinding anger.

And then, four nights after speaking with Cooper Shaye, as he sat alone at his drawing table, head hung low, his mind reeling with what his life would be like without Jillian, the phone rang.

"Arch Angel Enterprises. This is Jonas. How may I help you?" At first there was no reply, only silence. And then a voice spoke. A voice as soothing as a caress.

It was Lucias Angel.

And he wanted to see Jonas.

The meeting had been simple and short and never once while Angel was whispering dark promises to Jonas about returning his daughter to him did he ever think of Cooper Shaye and his warnings of a few nights earlier.

"I can bring her back to you, Jonas. Your little girl. Too young to die. A shame. She can be yours again." And Jonas, his heart crushed to powder from the sadness of watching Jillian slip away from him, never hesitated.

"What do I have to do?"

RETURN.

JONAS WATCHED THE FIRE, burning, burning, yellow, orange, black, burning. He turned quickly to Victor, whose eyes were moist with sorrow, fists clenched tight.

Jonas could read the expression in Victor's face as if he were speaking the words aloud, condemning him. *Who's the monster now?*, is what he was thinking.

"What choice did I have?" Jonas said so quietly it was but a whisper, nothing more than a plume of frost from his lips.

"There is always a choice," Victor said.

"Easy for a man to say who has hidden himself away from the world for two centuries. What kind of choice is that? You, more than anyone, should know how terrible the pain can sometimes become. How it can cripple you. Your mind. Make you do things you never dreamed possible."

Victor sighed, his bulk shifting beneath the flowing polar bear fur draped over him. "Have you finished gnashing your teeth because I don't think I could bear any more lecturing on pain and loss. Mine are enough—quite literally—to fill a book." He leaned forward, elbows on knees, the scar along his cheek flashing amber from the fire's flames. "Now are you going to finish telling me what happened? What you *did*, Jonas?"

"You know what I did," Jonas replied.

"Yes," said Victor, "But I want to hear you say it."

Jonas looked at Victor through vision blurred with the sting of tears. "Are you just being cruel now? You want to punish me?"

"You come here asking for my help and then you scramble upon your soapbox and dance away from the inelegance of the truth. Tell me what you have come to tell me or you can begin your walk back to the Inuit village. I'll even give you a torch to help fend off the bears."

Jonas closed his eyes, and images of Jillian immediately exploded beyond the field of his vision. But not the beautiful, glowing Jillian he had known all his life. Not the Jillian he would have died to protect. No, it was the Jillian that Lucias Angel had returned to him. Shambling. Empty-eyed.

"After Lucias Angel promised to bring her back, that he would help you, what did you do then, Jonas," Victor prompted. "What did you do then?"

Jonas slowly raised his eyes, bitterness flowing through him like acid. Through clenched teeth he said, "I brought her to him the next day."

THE JOURNEY ENDED.

THEY MOVED HER to one of the sub-basements of Arch Angel Enterprises and Jonas set up vigil. Round-the-clock nurses cared for her in a sterile room tucked away in a warren of secreted alcoves, dark places far from the public's prying eyes.

Her hands were like paraffin wax. Lifeless and dull. Jonas stroked the fallow skin to keep her warm. Soothe her. Provide any comfort he could as she slipped away from him. Then, on an autumn night as crisp and clear as the day she had entered the world, Jillian lowered her eyes and drifted into silence.

Jonas stroked her hair, tears burning his eyes like venom. After but a few minutes mourning, a nurse pulled him from his daughter and wheeled her from the room. "Time is of the essence," she said.

Jonas remained in the room for hours, alone, sobbing into hands that felt disconnected from his body.

Frail as a whisper, Jonas trudged home and spent the remainder of the night sitting in his living room, staring out the bay window into darkness. His vision blurred from the endless flow of tears, the world reeled out of focus. *What have I done*, he asked himself again and again. *Jesus Christ, what have I done?*

In the morning, he called Angel. In the afternoon he called again. That evening, his cell phone growing warm in his hand, he hit the redial button in a numbed haze. He never heard from the millionaire. The following morning he began the phone calls again. Two more days passed. Jonas did not go into work, he talked to no one.

And he never heard from Angel.

Four days after Jillian's death, Jonas returned to Arch Angel Enterprises. The building, its Gothic spires stabbing the bellies of storm clouds, sat blackened and cold. In the hundreds of windows that lined its face, only two burned with light. Jonas hunched his shoulders against the cold wind and made his way to the rear of the building. In the inky shadows beyond the employee entrance, he heard a familiar voice.

"I knew you were too weak," Cooper Shaye said. "I could see it in your eyes. Just like the rest."

Jonas dove for the homeless man, wrapping his fists around the threadbare collar of his sweatshirt. "What do you know about Jillian? What happened to her?"

Jonas struggled to remain stoic, to keep his facade of anger and strength but the tears welling in the pools of his eyes were already beginning to give him away.

"You know what happened to her," Shaye said. "Her father betrayed her."

"Please," Jonas pleaded, his hands falling away from Cooper Shaye's skeletal frame, dejected, defeated. "Tell me. Have you seen her?"

"They all end up down here on the streets, Jonas. All of them."

"Where is she? Take me to her."

"Why should I? So you can bring her more pain? You let the devil whisper in your ear and lure you into his bed."

"He said he could bring her back to me."

"Forget about her. Mourn her, cherish what you had with her. But move on. She is gone. You lost her the minute she drew her last breath. The dead should remain dead."

"I want to see her."

"She won't remember you. I tried to tell you. Lucias Angel says he can return the dead from their graves, but he can't. He can only return a shell—a portion of what that person was. We are his experiments."

Jonas squinted into the bruise-blue shadows. "You mean, you . . . you are . . ."

"Angel told my brother the same black lies he told you. And so here I am. But not all of me. Like I say, just a shell. Like a child's doll, a hardened exterior with sawdust inside. But I'm better than the rest, I suppose. Can at least form a sentence. Follow a single strand of logic for more than ten seconds. But the rest of them . . ."

"Take me to her," Jonas again pleaded. His voice had lost its resonance and his words came out in a tortured croak. "I'm begging you. I love her more than life itself. I . . . I was only trying to keep her with me."

There was a subtle shift in Shaye's coal dust eyes. A flicker of what Jonas could only describe as humanity. Compassion.

Shaye turned away, quietly. Not so much as a word. He made his way down the narrow alley leading back out into the sleeping heart of the city.

Jonas followed behind.

The Loop was preternaturally quiet. Like the hushed, eerie calm after a storm. During the day, the Loop pulsed with life. It was the financial heart of Chicago. But at night, the traders and lawyers all happily tucked away in their cozy suburban homes, the streets were deafeningly quiet.

Jonas could hear his own clacking footsteps ricocheting from the buildings.

They walked for several blocks, east toward the lake, the black ribbon of the Chicago River running beside them. In the center of Wacker Drive, enormous ramps sloped aggressively downward. Into darkness. Like hungry mouths agape.

Jonas knew at once where they were going. Beneath the streets of Chicago, through the darkened, greasy sub streets of Lower Wacker Drive, where scores of homeless people, ragged and brown with their own filth, scavenged for food and slept on flattened cardboard boxes atop steaming grates.

That's where they would find Jillian.

Jonas felt the familiar pinprick of shame and regret turn like a dull knife in his stomach. *No God*, he thought. *Not down here. She can't be down here.*

The ramp led Shaye and Jonas to the dark and corrupted streets of Lower Wacker, much warmer down here, away from the bracing winds, the steaming grates pumping dense moisture into the air.

"Why are we here, Shaye? Why would my little girl be down here? Amongst all the filth?"

"They all end up here, Burke. All of them. Tucked away from the city's prying eyes. To passersby they are just homeless trash. Transients and deviants to be ignored and disdained. Little do they suspect the dark and terrible secret they hold. That they have journeyed to the grave, and have returned. What do you suppose the typical three-piece-suited banker would think of that as he's merrily huffing off to work?"

Jonas did not hear Shaye's words. *Could* not hear them. His head buzzed as if hit by a downed power line. For in the distance . . .

. . . it was her.

She stood by a large metal garbage bin, a fire crackling within, painting her face a grotesque orange. Like a distorted Halloween mask.

Jonas began to cry, to openly weep. So happy was he to see his little girl again. Even in this corrupted state.

He went toward her, shrugging off Shaye's attempt to hold him back.

Some of the other shuffling undead scattered as he approached, cockroaches under the glare of a light.

"Jillian," he said. Quiet. A whisper.

And before she even looked up at him, before she even raised those midnight black eyes to gaze upon him from across the transom of death, Jonas Burke knew that Shaye was right.

It was Jillian. But, also, it was *not*. Not really.

She wasn't his little girl anymore. Not Jillian.

She was something else entirely. As if her body had been overcome by another being. Possessed.

Her eyes were shallow as pond water and deathly cold. Her skin was sodden and callow, milky-white and without luster. He could see instantly that she did not recognize him.

"Jillian," he said again, blankly.

She stared back at him, frozen. Jonas's heart seized up like a piston as he realized Jillian was paralyzed with fear. Afraid of *him*.

"I'm so sorry, Jillian. Please. I love you so much. Remember me. Please. Remember. It's me. It's daddy."

She yelped, a wordless holler. Nothing much more than a gurgling roar. And then she dashed away, the garbage bin nearly knocked onto its side in her haste.

Jonas watched in abject horror as his only daughter—the only thing remaining in this world—slipped away into the night.

"Your daughter is dead, Jonas Burke," the gravel voice of Shaye said. "And now she must forever roam these streets with the rest of us, Angel's rejects and failures, without memory, without love, without hope. You have doomed her to an existence of pain and futility. Your selfishness has done this. Everything good you brought into this world, you have destroyed. That is your legacy."

Long after Cooper Shaye had disappeared back into the shadows, Jonas stood in the mire of Lower Wacker Drive, the traffic thrumming over his head, retching until his stomach went dry and the tears in his eyes turned to nothing but dust.

AWAITING AN ANSWER.

HIS STORY CONCLUDED, Jonas fell to the ice, sobbing. He turned to Victor who sat motionless on his throne of ice, the Messiah of the North. Jonas looked for some measure of feeling in his eyes. Anything. Hatred. Revulsion. Perhaps sympathy.

But Victor's eyes were devoid of any hint of what he might be thinking.

Jonas lifted himself from the ice, his eyes raw, his teeth aching from clenching his jaw. He walked slowly toward Victor, toward the man everyone else in the world knew as a monster.

"They live in the streets like animals," he said. "Their bodies are whole, but their minds are feeble and frail. And I'm afraid that Lucias Angel will continue to spit them out. He'll keep trying. And when he fails, he will discard them. Nothing more than trash."

And then Jonas did something he could never have imagined himself doing. He laid a hand upon Victor's sleek and slender gloved right hand and pulled in close to the man, staring into the steel grey abyss of his eyes.

"Help me stop him, Victor. Help me stop Angel. To put an end to his experiments. I implore you. Not for me. But for all those poor creatures. The castaways and outcasts. They are . . . they are like you. Without home or family. Only pain."

With those words something shifted in Victor's eyes. What it was, Jonas could not be certain. But, hoping he had reached Victor's frozen and shielded core, he pressed on.

"What is your answer, Victor? Will you help me stop your brother?"

ICE BREAKER.

CAPTAIN EDWARD STACEY was ready to return home. There was a time when these forays "into the field" were the part of his job he enjoyed most. That was before Samantha had entered his life. And now, thirteen months after the wedding, little Gwen waited at home. Each passing day, each passing second, that he was away, he felt he was missing an important landmark in his daughter's development. More urgently, he was aware that the parental bonds that would hold his daughter close as long as they lived were being formed now. And there was no way to make up for lost time. That's why he had decided that this would be his last trip. He would talk to Simpkins when he returned to San Francisco and ask that he spend all his time in the lab, where he could be equally as valuable. If Simpkins declined, then Stacey would be left with no option but to resign.

He had been thinking about this course of action for some time. Had even discussed it with Samantha, but he had come to no conclusion until the hollow-cheeked stowaway, Jonas Burke, had been discovered below deck on the *Nostromo*. His story, no matter how unbelievable, had struck a nerve in Edward Stacey. Jonas Burke had watched every aspect of his life shatter around him, crash to the ground like a sand castle. Leaving him with the aching, corrosive regret that he did not have enough time.

Not enough time to spend with his daughter.

Stacey vowed that he would never harbor similar regrets. Gwen would come first.

He would miss standing at the bow of the *Nostromo*, the stillness of the North, the complete isolation and quietude. He would even miss the title despite the fact that it was but a formality. He was a scientist, not a captain, but Simpkins had insisted on the title in acknowledgement for his hard work. He would have preferred a raise, but the recognition was motivating—and gratifying—nonetheless. Stacey had worked for Natural Power, Inc. since graduating from Stanford twenty-two years earlier. All his adult life had been invested in searching for ways to improve the world's use of its natural resources. To reset the doomsday clock, as Samantha joked with him. It was work he enjoyed. Work he *loved*, but he could just as easily continue that work from his lab across the Golden Gate bridge, north of San Francisco in Point Reyes Station.

Turning his face into the wind, Stacey inhaled deeply, the crisp, cold air burning his nostrils. The *Nostromo* moved slowly forward, the constant creaking, cracking and snapping of the ice beneath its prow filling the eerie silence of the North Pole.

In the distance the Inuit village emerged from a thin bank of fog, thin tendrils of smoke trailing from the wooden shanties. As the ship pulled closer, slowing its speed as the crew prepared to drop anchor, he could see Jonas Burke, bundled in a dense tangle of seal skins, waving his arms wildly. Next to him, wrapped in a blinding white polar bear fur, was another man. Not an Inuit.

A man, just a shade taller than Jonas, with skin as white as the surrounding ice.

"Dear God," Edward Stacey said into the still air. "It cannot be."

THE PASSENGER.

THE *NOSTROMO* CRASHED through the endless sheets of Arctic ice like a saw sheering through bone. The ice cracked and splintered. Shattered like fingernails beneath a hammer. Inside her steel hull, beneath the tons of rivets and reinforced steel, the sound of the ice was constant, roaring in the ears of the crew members like a derailing freight train.

No one, except Captain Stacey, knew the identity of the *Nostromo's* new guest.

He was simply Victor.

The crew watched him from the corners of their eyes but would glance quickly away. They stared at the scars that pinched his skin and the sullen shrug of his shoulders. Jonas came to realize, however, that it was not Victor's physical abnormalities that drew attention and disquietude. Many of the crew barely noticed the odd color of his eyes and the flaccid pallor of his skin. But there was *something*. The men could feel it. Down to their bones. The same way they could feel the Arctic air grip them in its embrace.

None of them could put a name to it. It was simply a feeling. None could have known that their unease was due to the fact that, on some dark, primal level, they could feel the pull of the grave about their new visitor. A subconscious whispering in their heads told them that this man carried with him a perverse secret.

Many nervously offered their hands but Victor refused to shake them unless he was wearing gloves. Jonas never asked Victor why this was. But he was beginning to form an idea.

Each time a new crew member was introduced to Victor, his eyes would go wide and his words would trail out in a jumbled mess. Jonas tried to assign a word that best described the men's reactions. It was, quite simply, nothing more than rawboned fear.

Jonas realized that however they disguised Victor's physical differences, they could never camouflage the subtle terror he raised in people. The unsettling awareness of their own mortality that his gaze seemed to awaken. He walked and talked and looked every bit a man. But he was not. And all those who looked upon him sensed that. And it scared them ragged.

Sensing the discomfort he caused amongst the men, Victor shuttered himself away in his cabin for most of the remainder of the trip. He opened the door only for Jonas or Captain Stacey.

Jonas spent much of his time on the deck, as he had on the trip northward, staring out at the cold, dragon-green waters of the Pacific Ocean. After only a few short days the icebergs receded from view and the waters grew even darker. The air started to warm.

And on a sunny Saturday morning, seagulls hovering in the air like kites, the *Nostromo* edged toward Newfoundland's Great Saint Lawrence harbor. The ship docked overnight for supplies and pulled anchor again in the crisp hush of pre-dawn, the sky still as violet as a deep bruise.

When they dropped anchor again, two days later in Portland, Maine, Jonas turned to Victor and said simply, "This is it."

Jonas and Victor debarked quietly, leaving the crew to finish the last of their backbreaking chores before setting out by land for their final destinations. To families that awaited them, fires crackling in their hearths.

At the pier, Captain Stacey pumped Jonas's hand hard, as if he were saying farewell to the best friend he had ever known.

"How will you get back to Chicago?" the captain asked.

Jonas shrugged. "We'll find a way."

Stacey reached into his pocket and pulled out a crumpled wad of bills. "It's not much. About $200. It's all I have."

Jonas smiled. "Buy your wife a nice dinner. We'll be fine, captain."

Stacey kept the bills balled into one of his great ham fists.

"Have you found what you've come for, Jonas?" Stacey asked. "Will you find peace now?"

"Will you rest easier if I tell you 'yes'?"

The captain grinned his shaggy dog smile.

In the distance, at the far end of the pier, Victor waited, staring up at the sun as if seeing it for the first time. Stacey eyed him for a moment, sighed. "It can't really be him," he said. "It's impossible. Pure fantasy."

"And yet, you know it is him. You can feel it in your soul. Like a bolt of electricity."

"Yes, Jonas, but this . . . there is something ungodly about him. Some might say he transgresses the work of God."

"And others may argue the same about your ship, Captain. And microwave ovens, and open heart surgery, and computer games and pharmaceuticals."

Stacey smiled again, deep and warm. "Would I sound like a nagging wife if I were to tell you to be careful?"

"You're a bit hairy."

Stacey laughed. With a touch of somberness.

He lifted his hand, tried once again to ply the bills into Jonas's fist. Jonas stuffed his hand in his pocket.

"Take care of that little girl, Captain."

Then Jonas Burke turned away and walked stiffly down the concrete pier, toward the rising sun.

In Captain Edward Stacey's mind an image wavered. A little girl. Arms wide. Waiting to wrap them around his neck and smother him with kisses. Gwen. Dimpled and bathed in sunshine.

But, despite his best efforts, another image struggled darkly for his attention. Demanding to share space in his tired mind with that of his own daughter. And no matter how hard he fought to keep the mental image of his young daughter close at hand, another form took shape there. In the shadows.

It was a brooding man, with eyes as grey as a winter sky and the heaviness of the grave upon his heart. Edward Stacey realized, sadly, that it was an image he would carry with him for the rest of his life.

UNDER THE SKIN.

RAYMOND GRIMES'S FIRST REACTION as the knife slid into his belly was to laugh.

Of course, the man who had attacked him had no way of knowing that the blade was useless against him. No more dangerous than a child's toy.

Because Raymond Grimes was already dead.

Grimes's attacker's eyes narrowed, became faraway and opaque. When the man looked up into Grimes's ruined face, a silent scream formed on his lips.

"What the hell . . .?" the man said. Horror twisted his face. He tried to back away, his hand falling away from the knife that was impaled up to the hilt in Grimes's stomach.

Smiling a fleshless smile, Raymond Grimes knocked the man to the ground and stood over his fallen body. Grinning. Grinning.

They were on Lower Wacker Drive, hidden away beneath the city of Chicago, avenue after avenue drenched in darkness.

A long ramp, descending from Upper Wacker, led a few straggling commuters downward, sloping into this darkened, sunless maze. Few pedestrians ever ventured down the curving stairways that branched from the busy city streets. It was not a place for them, and they knew it in their bones.

Lower Wacker, and the surrounding roads, were replicas of the streets above them, but it was a fun-house reflection. A twisted twin of the world above.

The original intention of the urban planners was that this city beneath a city serve as a way to keep the constant flow of delivery trucks from clogging the city's roadways. But over the years it had been transformed into something else. A shelter for those who had nothing. A home for the homeless.

It served as refuge for an ever-growing army of people whom society had turned its back on. Unwashed, maimed, crippled, hungry. Humiliated. Many of them mentally incompetent. Many others simply without hope. They shuffled through the darkened streets beneath the city, warming themselves over trash can fires and eating whatever they could buy with the money they begged for, or failing that, whatever they could dredge up from the dumpsters that overflowed along the street.

The denizens of Lower Wacker shuffled through endless gloom, the neighboring Chicago River filling the air with the constant meaty tang of rotting fish and sewage.

Their moans—desperate and strained—provided a constant din as hunger gnawed at them day and night.

This was the world Raymond Grimes had come to inhabit.

And to hate.

He had no memory of how long he had been here. But it had been long enough. It was time to get out. And the only way he could do that was to become one of them. The surface dwellers. The businessmen hustling off to meetings, their ties dangling from their necks like dog collars. The shoppers, blissful and content in their consumption. The cops and traffic guards and sanitation workers who were perpetually on break.

To get out of the hell that Raymond Grimes had come to call home he would have to become like them. He would have to get beneath their skin. Or, more to the point, he would have to get a *skin* they would all recognize. One they would not turn away from in horror.

He had been one of them once. Many years ago. A cardiologist.

He had a beautiful wife. An even more beautiful mistress. Money to burn. But then that son of a bitch Seymour Cole had died on him during a routine triple bypass. Grimes had done more than a hundred of them in the course of his career. It should have been second nature.

But his nerves had been frayed that day, electrified by weeks of fighting with a wife and girlfriend who both demanded more than he was willing to give. A couple drinks was the only way to calm his nerves. By the time he realized he had clipped the old man's left anterior descending coronary artery, it was too late. Cole had thrown a blood clot that could stop a horse.

Grimes's lawyers spent more than two years—and all his money—trying to settle. But Cole's family would have none of it. The case finally went to trial and a doctor with a long history of struggling with the bottle never stood a chance. The jury came to a unanimous—and quick—decision that Grimes had in fact been negligent.

His medical license revoked, the hospital let him go, and his wife had no reason to stay once the social status of their marriage had been removed and naturally his mistress had no use for him once the money began to disappear.

Raymond Grimes turned increasingly toward the thing that had sent him on this downward spiral in the first place. The bottle. In the end, he was surprised at how quickly it could all be pissed away.

With debt weighing him down like an anchor and his social standing stripped bare, it was with a morbid resignation that Grimes first began to notice the swelling in his abdomen.

The nausea and fatigue set in quickly as his liver began to thicken and grow plump. At this stage he knew there was still time to turn the disease around, to come out on the other side alive and well. But Grimes had no desire. No will. He just wanted it to all be over.

When appetite loss turned to severe abdominal pain, he knew alcoholic hepatitis had set in, his liver inflamed, sickness burning through him like a brush fire. Still time to turn around, he told himself darkly, with a quiet laugh. Not fatal yet.

His drinking became even more voracious. The Grim Reaper was closing in and Grimes was anxious to see him face to face. To laugh at his skeletal visage.

The abdominal swelling was now met with a difficulty in breathing, which meant the Reaper was nearly upon him. Ascites had set in, Grimes knew. The final stages of cirrhosis. There was no going back now. The end was closing in, the final curtain being drawn.

The pain had grown so great that Grimes felt he was left with little choice. One night in early Autumn, sitting in a flea-bitten hotel room on the west side of the city, Grimes thought blackly of the 9mm Walther P99 laying silently in an old valise he kept tucked under the bed. He imagined the cold metal against his teeth, the barrel resting gently on the curve of his tongue.

That's when the phone rang.

In his younger days, when he had the world firmly by the balls, Raymond Grimes had been the first name to call for those wealthy enough to afford his services. He was the best, simply put. It was back in those glory days that Lucias Angel had called in a favor or two. Not for Angel himself, of course; he had his own cadre of private physicians and he trusted absolutely no one outside his inner circle for his own medical needs. But he had a few generals below him, middle managers to the core, who needed Grimes's special skills. And, for a price, he was all too willing to accommodate.

That had been many years ago, and he had not heard from Angel in well over a decade.

Until now.

His voice, as sonorous and mild as a pool of honey, came to him from the other end of the line. And he told Grimes that he could make him whole again. Make him complete. No more liver damage. No more sickness.

He could return him to his former glory.

All he had to do was forego the gun he was contemplating ("So very messy," Angel had whispered) and open his nightstand drawer.

Grimes pulled open the drawer, hands palsied from his sickness, expecting to see nothing more than the Gideon Bible he had already ignored a hundred times. But instead he saw a plastic bottle, filled with thick white pills.

"Take them all, Raymond. It will be quick. And when you return, the world will be yours again."

In the end, he didn't do it because of Angel's promises. It was simply that a gun took too much courage. It had a sullen finality that frightened him. The pills were easier, painless.

He simply drifted off to sleep.

And woke up . . . here. Underneath the city like some discarded piece of trash.

Alive. But *not* alive.

Surrounded by the other shuffling failures of Arch Angel Enterprises. Only he was different. Special. With the exception of Cooper Shaye he was the only one who could even form a complete sentence. And even Shaye had problems remembering things.

Raymond Grimes was the only one of Angel's children who had all his faculties intact. The rest were bumbling cretins, mush-brained zombies that skittered about the black streets like rats. But Grimes's mind was as strong as it had ever been; it remained the brain of a brilliant surgeon.

But his *body*.

That was something else entirely.

The other creatures that had been coughed from Angel's labs were feeble-minded, their brains scattered and muddled. But there bodies, at least, were intact.

Raymond Grimes, for better or worse, was the exact opposite. His mind was diamond sharp. As precise as a finely tuned violin.

But his body was failing him, decomposing before his very eyes, melting back into the earth from which it had come. Grimes had been reanimated like the others, but his flesh continued to rot, peeling away in strips like worn wallpaper. A few fatty knots of blackened skin remained here and there but mostly he was nothing but tendons and meaty red cartilage. A walking, talking anatomy model.

At one time he had grown to accept his fate; his body tattered and ruined he would live in the darkened underbelly of the city like a cockroach.

But no longer.

In the long, dark hours of his exile, a simple question began to form in his mind. Why hadn't Angel and his minions destroyed their failed experiments instead of turning them out into the streets? Why not simply return them to death's embrace, burn them back to dust?

The answer, Grimes came to realize, is that the experiments were not over when the dead were reanimated. Angel set them free for one simple reason—to see which of them would *return*. It was a test. A gauntlet to run.

And Grimes would be the first to prove his worth. He would walk triumphantly through the doors of Arch Angel Enterprises, a modern day Lazarus, a man for whom even the grave could not hold.

But in order to see that vision come to fruition, he needed to get the hell out of here.

He needed to return to the surface. To the world above.

And he couldn't do it with a face like this.

The man who had attacked him, who had mistakenly thought he would be an easy mark, was still sprawled on the sidewalk at his feet. The man was paralyzed with fear, staring up at the desecrated flesh of Grimes's face, his bare teeth exposed like those of a skeleton.

Raymond Grimes realized it was time to once again put his skills to use. The hands of a surgeon, after all, should never go to waste. It was a crime against the creator.

He grabbed the handle of the knife, the blade still sunk up to its hilt in his stomach, and slowly pulled it free. The blade slid loose with a wet, thick slurp. The sound of a foot being pulled from the mud. The man on the ground whimpered, childlike.

Once free, the knifeblade glistened pink from the fluids in Grimes's skinless body.

The man who had attacked him was clearly a Breather. Most likely an addict, hoping to shake Grimes free of a few loose coins. The man was not a product of Angel's labs. He was *alive*.

Which meant he could be of use to Grimes. He could help set the wheels in motion to get him out of this place.

The man's skin was dirty, but it was fresh. It looked soft and it was pink with color, rosy red.

Grimes pressed the knife against the man's throat. "I am going to need you to be quiet," he said. "Can you do that? If not, this could get a whole lot worse for you." But to be certain, Grimes stuffed his balled fist into the man's mouth, soft teeth caving inward.

As he dragged the knife across the flesh beneath the man's chin a black-red fissure of blood cascaded over the blade. The man twitched and writhed, his screams muffled.

This will be easy, Raymond thought. *I'll get beneath their skin. I'll become one of them.*

CONFRONTATION.

JOE HADLEY STACKED THE BILLS neatly into piles. Ones. Fives. Tens. Twenties. Every so often a fifty or even a C-note would find its way into his register, but not today. Washington, Lincoln, Hamilton and Jackson stared up at him, imperious, blank-eyed.

He had made his way down to the diner early this morning for no other reason than he could not sleep. The clock above the kitchen door, a smiling black cat, its tail ticking the seconds away, read 6:35 when he came in.

It was now ten past seven. Joe expected no one for another forty-five minutes. It was a good time to cash out the register, something he should do each evening—like his father had done every day since he started the ButterCup Diner back in the fifties until his passing just two years back—but it was work Joe did not relish. In fact, there was nothing about his responsibility at the ButterCup Diner that could convince Joe he wouldn't be better off packing his bags and heading west, into the heat of the sun. The winters in Chicago were more than simply brutal. They were monstrous, taking on a life of their own. The wind and snow and bitter, bone-freezing cold could drive a man to the brink of unreason.

But he would never be able to convince Eunice to leave. She had family here stretching back generations. She had already told Joe in no uncertain terms that if he planned on leaving Chicago's south side in his rearview mirror, he was going to do it alone.

Of course, even if he had been able to gather the courage to pursue his dream of abandoning this two-bit diner, what in the world would he do then? He was nearing seventy, his brown skin webbed with wrinkles, his hearing dim and his eyesight cloudy, and this was the only job he had ever held. The only life he had ever known. And he wasn't qualified in the least to do anything else.

Thirty-three, thirty-four, thirty-five, thirty-six. He put a rubber band around the stack of ones and put them in a brown paper bag. He stuffed it beneath the counter.

The stack of fives did not take long. Only five. Twenty-five lousy bucks. "I'll be Goddamned," he muttered. He counted the tens next; three-hundred-ten dollars. He bundled the fives and tens together and slipped them into the bag.

That left only the tiny stack of Stonewall Jacksons on the counter. Joe fanned them out. Shook his head. Four of them. Eighty dollars. Plus the three-hundred-ten, plus the twenty-five, plus the—he couldn't remember exactly how many singles there had been—but maybe altogether it came to five hundred bucks.

"I'll be Goddamned," he muttered again, louder.

That's how much those restaurants up along the Gold Coast made every ten seconds.

Joe poured himself a cup of coffee, and when the bell above the door began to tingle he nearly spit his first sip down the front of his shirt.

Two men stepped in.

"Sweet Moses. You boys nearly put me in the ground." Joe put his glad-to-see-ya smile on. The one his father had taught him back when he was only eight, first working the diner after school and on the weekends.

"You fellas here to eat, or just grab a cup of java?"

"Eat."

"You're in luck. Don't usually open for another half hour or so." Joe led them to a booth and laid a menu in front of both of them.

"I'll bring you some water, give you a sec to look over the menu. Cook everything myself. All homemade."

Joe returned to his cup of coffee and from behind the counter watched the two men. He would wait a minute or two before bringing their water to them. The stench of the two men still burned in Joe's nose. He couldn't get away from them fast enough.

They were both filthy, streaked with mud. Their clothes were dank and musty. One of them, the one who had spoken, devoured the menu, scouring every inch as if he were engrossed in a great book. The other did not move.

And there was something about him that Joe did not like. Did not like at all.

He was tall and thickly built. He wore a thick coat of white fur. His skin was yellow-white, like milk that had turned. And he had a scar that ran across his forehead. His eyes were as cold and gray as a winter sky.

These two certainly weren't from this part of town and he didn't want them around when his bleary-eyed regulars arrived.

He scooped ice into two glasses, poured water from a pitcher behind the counter and brought them to the table.

"What can I get you fellas?"

The one with the scar did not speak, did not even flinch.

The other one had a feral intensity to his eyes, like he had not eaten in days. "Two eggs," he said. "Over easy. With three buttermilk pancakes and a side of white toast."

"Yes, sir, and how about you?" he asked the man in the blinding white coat.

"Nothing," he said.

"Alright then. I'll have your order right up."

Joe stepped through the swinging set of double doors that led into the kitchen. On the back wall he had three copies of wanted posters taped crookedly into place. They were grainy; copies of copies of copies. Even after mentally removing the facial hair from the men—two with full beards, the other a thick handlebar mustache—they did not even remotely resemble either of his new customers.

Joe cracked two eggs into a skillet and poured out three even mounds of pancake batter. He set them to low heat and hushed back through the kitchen doors. Standing behind the counter, he continued his vigil over the two men. He busily shuffled napkins and straightened menus, his head bowed and eyes rolled upward, trying to remain discreet and unnoticed as he watched.

Five decades in the diner had taught Joe to be tirelessly on guard, and these two radiated bad feelings in Joe's gut like a meal that had gone sour. He had been robbed only twice in all those years—both at gunpoint—and he had no intention of letting that happen again. At least not without a fight.

Scar-Face sat stone still, his gray eyes fixed straight ahead. The other one fidgeted and twisted his hands like he was trying to wring water from them. He was anxious, agitated, scratching his stubbled white hair and tapping the table with his fork, but Joe felt no threat from him.

Scar-Face, however, was a different story. The man chilled Joe through and through. And it was not just his appearance that set Joe on edge—the milky scar, skin the color of spent candle wax—there was something more. The coldness of the man's eyes was not simply a manifestation of boredom or indifference. Within that heart there lied a terrible secret. Joe sensed it, felt it like a whisper at the back of his neck.

Rubbing his arms for heat, he stepped back into the kitchen and reappeared minutes later with a dishwasher-spotted white plate holding the eggs, three pancakes and a twig of garland. He paused for a moment and shot a glance toward the darkened cubbyhole beneath the cash register.

From its shadows he caught a heartbeat glint of light off metal. When his eyes turned back upward, the feral glare of Scar-Face standing before him made his knees buckle and he nearly lost hold of the plate.

He flashed a quick mock smile. "Jesus. Nearly gave me a stroke."

"My friend is very hungry."

"Alright, keep your pants on. I'm on my way. Say, you boys never did tell me where you're from."

"Up North," he said

"Oh yea. Where abouts? Twin Cities?"

"Little further. Can we get that food now?"

"Sure thing, didn't mean to keep you waiting."

Joe walked past Scar-Face, and for a moment his breath caught in his throat. It was like someone had opened a door on a black winter's night. He turned back around, quickly, just a glance, and looked into the dark well of those gray eyes.

"Something wrong?" Scar-Face asked.

"Nothing. Nothing," Joe said turning away, anxious about having his back to the man but more anxious to get away from him. He fumbled the plate and it clanged onto the table.

"Thank you," the white-haired man said before tearing into the meal. At this rate he would be finished before Joe returned from the kitchen with his toast.

Scar-Face crashed back down into his seat at the booth, and Joe hurried back behind the counter. He put one hand on the swinging doors to the kitchen, like a gunfighter pausing before entering the saloon. He stared over at the cash register again, and then down at the counter.

"I'll be Goddamned," he said under his breath.

When the men had entered the ButterCup, Joe had just about finished counting up yesterday's receipts. He had bagged the ones, fives and tens, but the twenties he had just fanned out across the countertop when the bell above the door started jangling. He remembered it plain as day. He had left eighty dollars sitting on that counter, and now it was gone. He retrieved the paper bag from under the counter, just to be certain. The twenties were not there.

He quickly darted his hands into his pants pockets. Nothing.

Joe's temples throbbed. Think. Think. He fumbled into the kitchen and brought the toast to the famished man. He had devoured all three pancakes and most of the eggs. Joe slid the plate onto the table without saying a word and stepped back behind the counter.

His hands trembled as he reached into the darkness of the cubbyhole. He recoiled at first as his flesh touched the cold metal; then he embraced it. Withdrew it like a baby from the womb, leaving only darkness behind. The smiling cat clock ticked away the seconds above Joe's head.

He tucked the .38 snub-nose into his waistband. His forehead was beaded with sweat, even though he was still chilled to the core. His hands, trembling more violently now, had gone numb.

He plopped heavily onto a stool behind the register, crashing downward as if he had been dropped from the heavens. He could feel the weight of the gun pressing against his stomach. Could feel its cold urgency.

Joe waited.

It was not long. The two men came toward him. The hungry man, his eyelids droopy and sated, reached into his pocket and pulled out a five-dollar bill. He laid it on the counter and smoothed it with his hand.

"Your menu said the eggs and pancake breakfast is $2.59. I hope this will be enough."

Joe could feel the veins in his forehead throb, the blood rushing. He fought to control his hands. "Maybe your friend could lend you some money."

"This is all we have. It should be enough. Your menu said . . ."

"He might have more than you think," Joe said. "Why don't you ask him what he was doing up at this counter when I came out of the kitchen. When he scared me half to death. Ask him."

"I don't know what you are talking about," the white-haired man said.

Scar-Face remained silent, and that incensed Joe even further. Say something. Defend yourself, Goddamn it. He fumbled for the gun, tugged at it viscously. It was snagged. He twisted it sideways, and he could see the brief electric-flash spark of fear shimmer in the hungry man's eyes. He took a step backward, then as Joe continued to wrestle the gun from his waistband, another. Scar-Face remained still and silent.

Even after Joe finally pulled the gun free and leveled it at his head, the big man did not move. Not so much as a blink or twitch.

"Now, I know you don't want to die over eighty bucks. Surely, your life is worth more than that."

"What the hell are you talking about?" the hungry man screamed.

"Your friend knows. Don't you, son? Now hand it over. I won't call the cops; I won't do a damn thing. This is between us. I just want my money back."

"Put the gun down," Scar-Face said flatly.

Joe's hands were trembling furiously now. He hated that he could not control it, that he had to show such weakness to these two men.

"Put the gun down," repeated Scar-Face, this time through clenched teeth. More trembling. Scar-Face's eyes turned the color of stormclouds, a thick, ominous silver-gray. Joe felt faint.

Scar-Face took a step toward him, asked him again to put the gun down. Joe cocked the hammer. "Don't come any closer," he warbled and suddenly realized that he was no longer the hunter, he was the prey. He was backing up, falling over his own feet, while Scar-Face pressed closer and closer to him. Anything that happened now was a clear-cut case of self-defense.

"Let's get the hell out of here," the hungry man pleaded, but his friend continued to lumber toward Joe who was now backed up against the wall and had nowhere left to turn. He was out of options. As Scar-Face reached for him—with a huge, hammer-sized fist—he pulled the trigger. The pale white flesh of Scar-Face's hand settled over his wrist, clasped it tight and in that moment Joe's mind collapsed in upon itself.

He could feel himself continue to pull the trigger. Could hear the cracking of the gun's report. But it was as if these things were happening at a distance or to someone else entirely.

Joe was no longer in the ButterCup diner. He was standing over a bed, a thin, frail form strewn out before him.

"My God. Eunice? Is that you?"

It was clearly Eunice and yet . . . it couldn't be. She was bone-thin, her once vibrant skin the color of chalk. Her chest heaved up and down from the air being forced into her lungs from the respirator at her side, a tube taped to her still mouth.

"No, no. Eunice. No!"

Sweet Jesus. What was happening? This couldn't be real. He reached out for Eunice's emaciated hand. Just to hold her one last time before she left him forever. But he could not move. He was frozen. Paralyzed.

Joe Hadley screamed.

And screamed.

When his eyes opened, he could see the tail on the cat clock wagging back and forth. He was on his back, behind the counter, slathered in oily sweat. His eyes were dry, his tongue stuck to the roof of his mouth.

He pulled himself to his feet. He briefly closed his eyes to fight off a wave of nausea but the image of Eunice lying on her death bed, her body turned into something corrupt and horrible, wavered in his mind. A terrifying mirage he could not control. He forced his eyes open again, sharply.

The two men, of course, were gone. Joe must have fainted. Slowly the memory of the gunshots came back to him.

Like a newborn colt, weak-kneed and wobbly, he got to his feet. He shuffled across the diner, to where the men had been seated. He looked at the wall above the booth.

"I'll be Goddamned," he whispered.

Gingerly he put his finger into one of the six holes left by the .38 caliber bullets. The hole was still warm.

Impossible, Joe thought. He was standing right in front of me. I must have hit him with *something*.

Back behind the counter he checked his paper bag, just to be certain the thieves had not discovered it on their way out. The ones, fives and tens were all there.

Joe called the police department, told them of the robbery, and then fell back onto the stool. He rubbed his temples. He tried not to blink. Even closing his eyes for a second brought back those dark images, those creeping, horrifying glimpses of Eunice's death. He reached into his front shirt pocket for his pack of Marlboros. He was still trying to quit—had gotten down to just more than a pack a week—but he needed a smoke now. Concern for his health could wait.

He pulled the half-spent box from his pocket and as he did so four twenty-dollar bills, old Stonewall Jackson staring smugly up from the finger-smudged surfaces, fluttered to the floor.

"I'll be Goddamned," Joe said.

AN OLD FRIEND.

JONAS AND VICTOR stood in the waning evening light, amidst the bustle of Chicago's financial district, as tired commuters rushed to catch homeward trains. They walked against the flow of people, pushing, bumping, shoving. North on LaSalle Street.

The winter sun, distant and gray, dipped behind the city's towering skyscrapers.

Jonas sighed. At long last, he was back in Chicago. Back *home*.

They had hitchhiked their way out of Maine (with a barrel-chested, red-bearded trucker named Daryl) during a pre-dawn thunderstorm that followed them for days.

All through New Hampshire and Vermont and New York State and Pennsylvania and Ohio, they sleepwalked from bus station to truck stop to rest area, catching rides from an array of faceless ciphers, crisscrossing America, all with their own desperate stories to tell.

Finally, in Lima, Ohio, nearly a full week after stepping from the *Nostromo*, they piled into the rust-weary Ford Pinto of a baby-faced art student returning to Columbia College Chicago after a short break, and shimmied and sputtered all the way through central Indiana, up I-94 as it skirted the southern edge of Lake Michigan until finally coming to rest on the city's south side.

Right in front of a place called the ButterCup Diner and a "welcome home" that had included a gun pointed at their chests. Jonas hoped the events of the morning were not a foreboding glimpse into things to come.

As Jonas and Victor approached the Chicago River, the crowds began to thin. The enormous crush of people—not individuals, but a pulsating mass—tapered into a trickle. A few Burberry-coated men dashed blindly across crosswalks without looking for traffic. *Can't miss the train. Can't be late.*

A gaggle of middle-aged women wobbled under the weight of their shopping bags from *Lord & Taylor*, *Crate & Barrel*, *Nieman Marcus* and *Macy's* (although to a true ice-blooded Chicagoan like Jonas, the sprawling State Street store would always be known as *Marshall Field's*).

Victor walked haltingly, his head constantly turned skyward, his mouth agape like a child's. He had never seen a skyscraper, at least not in person. Only in books. He was overwhelmed by the magnificence of the buildings, their sheer glass-and-metal power. They crossed over the Chicago River and walked two blocks north until they reached a building so sleek and dark it looked to have been carved from obsidian.

They entered the lobby, huge and sprawling, Italian marble reflecting the overhead lights back at them like a blanket of stars. A crisp guard stood behind a semicircle of polished marble.

"May I help you?" he asked stiffly.

"We're waiting for someone," Jonas replied.

"Most everyone's gone by now, sir."

"He's not."

"May I ring him for you, sir?"

"We'll wait."

Jonas led Victor to a set of four plush chairs in the corner of the lobby. A coffee table, polished chrome and shining steel, held dozens of copies of *Medicine Today*, dating back more than a year, fanned out like a peacock's tail.

Neither man sat. Instead they both looked out onto the sidewalk in front of the building. Watching the last remaining stragglers blindly careening through traffic like toy pieces.

"Maybe he's not here," Victor offered blandly.

"He's here."

The guard shot occasional distrustful glances over at the two men, flashing the kind of narrow-eyed look Jonas had become accustomed to over the course of the past weeks. Jonas was unshaven, his prickly beard growing in as white as the marble of the lobby's floor. He looked disheveled, unkempt, ragged from so much time on the road. He needed a bath. The look of the guard told him as much.

At the opposite end of the lobby there sat a long bank of elevators. The first half carried passengers from the ground floor through the thirty-fourth; the second half began at floor thirty-five and discharged riders as high as the penthouse on the eighty-second floor. A quiet ding interrupted the silence of the lobby, and the doors of one of the elevators hushed open.

A thin man, his blue pinstriped suit tailored to perfection, stepped off the elevator, a brown briefcase in his right hand. He walked crisply through the lobby, his shoes click clicking as he marched across the marble.

"Good night, Preston," he said to the guard.

"Night, Mr. Wallace. You have a nice evening."

He was almost to the revolving door leading to the street before he noticed the two men standing in the lobby. He smiled uncomfortably in their direction and heaved against the door.

"Walton," Jonas called out, his voice ricocheting through the high-ceilinged lobby like a gunshot.

Walton stepped back. He peered over toward Jonas and Victor. He squinted.

"Did you call me? Do I know you?"

Jonas moved toward him. Slowly. Smiling. "Have you made partner yet?"

Walton squinted harder, squeezed his eyes tight, his face crinkling like a puppy's. His eyes suddenly shot wide, mouth opened as if he was gasping for air. "Jonas?" He stepped toward him. "It can't be. Jonas," he said again.

He hugged Jonas Burke, and Jonas hugged him back, wrapping his arms around him and pounding him on the back. Walton grabbed him by the shoulders and looked into his eyes. "What in the hell happened to you? I thought . . . Jesus, I don't know what I thought. I can't believe you're here."

"I'm here, and I've brought a friend."

Suddenly, Victor was beside them, appearing as if from behind a puff of smoke, a cheap magician's trick.

"This is Victor," Jonas said.

Walton held out a hand, but Victor did not shake it.

Walton smiled awkwardly, stuffed his hand hesitantly into a front pocket and turned back toward Jonas.

"It's so good to see you," Walton said.

"It's good to see you too, buddy. Listen, I hate to cut right to the chase . . ."

"Go ahead. What's on your mind?"

Jonas still smiled. "I need a little favor."

SMELLING THE ROSES.

UNABLE TO SLEEP, Walton Wallace pulled on a pair of black slippers and shuffled into the kitchen. Twisted dreams, filled with corrupted human flesh, tugged him awake time and again. Unrelenting.

He lifted a glass from the kitchen sink, rinsed it quickly, and filled it with milk from a quart tucked away at the back of the refrigerator. The milk was cold, too cold. It set his teeth on edge. He set the glass back in the sink and headed into the darkened living room.

He had promised Jonas that he would ask no questions, that he would not needle him for explanations, but that promise was already beginning to make him feel uneasy. There was something about Jonas's friend that was not right. Something that disturbed and frightened Walton deeply. Touching a dark place within him he barely knew existed.

"Can't sleep?"

Walton felt his heart freeze, and despite his best attempts, a small, pitiful squeal escaped him. He reached for the light switch on the wall. The overhead light, dull and strangely yellow, flickered to life.

"Jesus Christ. You scared the shit out of me."

Victor sat in the corner of the room, in an old Victorian reading chair that had belonged to Walton's grandfather.

"Forgive me," he said.

"How long have you been sitting out here in the dark?"

"I do not heed much attention to time. It has never been one of my great interests."

Walton crossed the room and sat on the edge of the sofa. He leaned back, but for some reason it felt too informal in front of this stranger. He leaned forward again.

"Can't sleep either, huh?" Walton said.

"Sleeping has also never been one of my great interests."

"What *are* your interests?"

"I am afraid you would find them quite pedestrian."

"You want something to drink? Bite to eat, maybe?"

Victor shook his head.

What was it about this man that was so disquieting, Walton wondered. The scarring on his face was certainly pronounced, but it in no way made him look monstrous. Maybe it was his skin; deathly white and pallid. Or perhaps the eyes; gray and cold and deep. Whatever it was, Walton was glad that he was leaving for Baton Rouge in the morning on business. When he returned in four days, Jonas had promised the two men would be gone. He felt no trepidation whatsoever about allowing them to stay in his home while he was away; he could trust Jonas Burke with his life. He knew that. His old friend would never allow anything to happen while he was gone.

Suddenly it occurred to Walton that Victor was still wearing his fur coat. "Want me to turn the heat up?" he asked.

"No. Thank you. Your hospitality has been most kind."

Walton scratched his head and stretched, a tingling exhaustion settling in behind his eyes.

"Victor, can I ask you a question?"

"Of course." Victor had not so much as twitched a muscle since Walton had entered the room. He was as still as stone.

"You two aren't in any trouble, are you? I've known Jonas for years. Since we were snot-nosed kids. He's always been the responsible one. Talking me off the relationship ledge time and again. Knocking some sense into me about my career, the path I was on. But now . . . it's just that . . . the way he looks now, shit, I didn't even recognize him. I know what happened with Jillian was devastating to him, but . . . I'm just concerned. That's all. Just tell me I shouldn't be."

Not only had Victor not moved, but Walton was positive that he had not even blinked. Not once. "I wish that I could give you such reassurance. But I'm afraid I do not know Jonas half as well as you do."

"But you are traveling together; you must know something about him."

"I know that he has made an error in judgment that has cost him dearly. And through that error in judgment, he has come to know me."

"He hasn't hurt anybody, has he?"

Victor did not answer. "Mr. Wallace, I'm sure you know that you are having this conversation with the wrong person. But seeing as you have asked me many questions, perhaps you will allow me to ask one of you in turn. Do you have any books in your home?"

"Books?"

"To read. Do you have anything to read?"

"I have some old *National Geographics*. And there's this girl, Veronica or Virginia, I don't remember, but she kinda has a thing for me, she sent me a book in the mail. She works a couple floors above me, in accounting I think, but I've already got a girlfriend. I never even picked the thing up. It's right here." Walton huffed from the couch and went back into the kitchen. The book sat atop the counter, never moved since the day he opened it three weeks ago. He carried it to Victor.

"It's the new Patterson. Ever read him?"

Victor set the book down on the floor at his feet without even looking at it. "I'll take the *National Geographics*, if you don't mind."

"They're in the can. Help yourself."

Victor did not move. "Perhaps I can ask you another question?"

Walton sat back down on the couch. The uneasiness was creeping back into him again. This man was too still, too stoic. He was like a Goddamn statue, he thought.

"What did you do today?"

"What do you mean?"

"Tell me about your day. What you did. The people you met. What you saw. The smells. The sounds."

"I don't understand."

Victor's eyes narrowed; it was the first movement Walton had been able to detect since joining him in the living room. "I've been away for a long time. I want to know what life is like here in the city. In Chicago. Tell me."

"Not much to tell. Had breakfast . . ."

"Where?" Victor interrupted.

"Here. In the kitchen. Wasn't much of a meal. Bowl of Cheerios. I didn't even sit down; I just gulped it down standing over the sink. I was running late. What else is new, right?"

"Then you did what?"

"Went to work."

"Tell me how you got there."

Walton laughed, and as soon as he did he felt regret. This man, this stranger, was serious. Walton pushed the peculiarity of the questions from his mind and continued. "The train. The 'L'. Drops me just a few blocks from work."

"Then you walk from there?"

"Sure. Or take a cab when it's raining. But today it was nice."

"What did you see?"

"Do you mind me asking why you want to know this? It's not the most interesting stuff in the world."

"My curiosity has always been a weakness. Indulge me."

Walton closed his eyes for a moment and tried to conjure in his mind a picture of what it was he saw each day on the way to work. He was amazed how difficult it was. Every day for eleven years he had taken the same route to work. Every day for eleven years he had walked down the same streets, passed the same shops, probably even seen the same people. Yet now, when questioned about it, he could recall almost none of it.

"There's a bakery. It's on the corner. One of the highbrow places where a cup of coffee sets you back four dollars. Muffins with apricots and kiwi and organic oats and shit like that in them."

"What does it smell like? Can you remember?" Victor leaned forward; the chair squeaked. My God, Walton thought, the statue moves.

"It's a great smell. Fresh-baked bread. Thick yeast. I don't know how to explain it."

"What else do you see?"

Walton closed his eyes again. "A camera store. A deli; no, that's gone. It used to be a deli. What is it now? A Walgreen's maybe. There's also a shoe store and a music shop, the kind that gives lessons." Walton shrugged. "That's all I can remember."

"How about the sounds of the street. What do you hear?"

Walton laughed. "Honking, yelling, car engines, screeching tires. Never a second of silence."

"Until but a few days ago I had never heard such sounds. Amazing sounds. What did you do at work? Describe your day to me."

"Boredom. Meetings, deadlines, disgruntled customers. Same thing day in and day out."

"Something of interest must have happened."

"It's work, Victor. Nothing of interest ever happens. More than a decade ago I left my medical practice for life in the fast lane of medical management, tilting at windmills every day, lobbying for changes in the healthcare system. Jonas tried to talk me out of it. Said I would miss the personal interaction with patients. That I would miss practicing damn medicine. And like always, he was right."

"Did you take a break? Go for a walk perhaps?"

Walton laughed again. "Not to be unkind, Victor, but where are you going with these questions? I don't know what it is you want from me. I ate lunch at my desk, as I always do. Made a quick call to my girlfriend. Other than . . ."

"Girlfriend? Tell me of her."

"What?"

"Do you love her?"

"Man, you really know how to get to the heart of things."

"Do not tell me if you feel uncomfortable."

"No. It's not that. It's just . . . I don't suppose I've thought that much about it. Her name is Judith. I met her at the office. She was a temp at the time. Now she's working for the city."

"And you enjoy the time you spend together?"

"She's very pretty."

"Pretty. Is that all?"

"No. That was stupid. Of course, it's much more than that. She's sweet. Like no one I've ever known before. I guess part of me feels like maybe she's too good to be true. You know what I mean?"

Victor stared back at Walton, eyes dark as death. "Do I know the sting of rejection from a lover?" he said. "Yes . . . yes."

"Anyway, maybe . . . maybe we'll settle down together. I guess that sounds pretty good right about now."

Victor's dark eyes shifted, like a sky riven by lightning. "What else, Walton? What else can you tell me? "

"Jesus, Victor. Other than lunch the only break I took was to go to the can. There's nothing to tell you. Every day I go to work; I'm tired and not too excited to get there so I don't notice the buildings around me and I don't stop to listen to the sounds and I could give a shit about the smells. There isn't enough time. I'm sorry if that sounds terrible to you."

The man leaned forward, and for a moment, although he could not say why, Walton thought Victor was going to lunge for him, attack him. Walton pulled away. He felt his heart flutter, wither and grow small for just a moment. For the first time he noticed the two different sized hands, one small and bony, the other as big as a mallet. Walton was beginning to regret his sarcasm.

"I have very few pleasant memories," Victor said, his voice as soft as a breeze. "Most are of pain and ice and neglect and abandonment, but there is one that never fails to warm me when I think of it. It was many years ago, in the Swiss Alps outside the University of Ingstoldt. I was alone, walking through hills that swelled up around me like the waves of an ocean. Everything was green, lush. The sun shone bright and warm. I took off my clothes. Naked, I laid down upon the grass."

For a moment Walton thought he could discern the faintest whisper of a smile on Victor's scarred face. "And that's it? You just laid there?"

Victor nodded. "The grass was cool beneath me, the sun warm above. I rolled over. The grass embraced and caressed me. The sun soothed and comforted me. If I had been allowed to stay, I should have done that every day, I thought."

"Take off your clothes and roll around in the grass?" Walton fought the urge to laugh again, but he knew better. "I know what you saying, Victor. Don't think I don't. But there's no time anymore. No time for anything. You know what I mean? Run here, run there. Never time to even collect your thoughts. I suppose it wasn't always that way. I'm sure there were simpler times, as you hear people talk about, but those days are gone." Walton shrugged. Then he smiled, in spite of himself. "I'm sorry, Victor; I don't mean to take what you've told me lightly, but . . . I mean, that's the only pleasant memory you have? Lying in the grass? Explain that to me."

Victor's pallid, scarred face remained flat and lifeless. And then, quietly, he said, "It was the only time I can ever remember feeling alive."

The limo to take Walton to the airport pulled up in front of his building at 6:10 in the morning. Sleepy-eyed, Walton huffed his suitcase into the trunk and settled into the back seat of the stretch sedan. He closed his eyes, and just before he drifted off to sleep, as the car pulled out into the early morning traffic, he had the sensation of lying unclothed in a field of emerald green grass that stretched to the horizon, the sun warming him deeply, soothing him to his very soul, while the cool grass beneath him caressed and lulled him into a watery bliss.

(ANOTHER) OLD FRIEND.

DR. RAYMOND GRIMES had forgotten how much he missed the cutting.

Scalpel slicing through skin, skin peeling back to expose tendon, tendon relinquishing to cartilage, cartilage finally giving way to bone.

It made him feel strong. *Alive.*

But it was delicate work. It was not intended for brutes. It required grace, wisdom, patience. And a steady hand.

There was a beauty in the cutting. Every doctor knew it, and yet it was something none of them would discuss. Never. Not even with one another. People would not understand. They would find it ghoulish and gruesome. But the dark truth of the matter was that every doctor felt it. A black urge at the edge of their reason. They wanted to heal, yes. To cure, yes. To discover.

But sometimes, they just wanted to revel in the cutting. And no one knew this more than Raymond Grimes.

At first he had a very clear mission in mind. A goal to strive toward. Using his capable hands, he was going to rebuild himself. Graft skin where there was none. And soon enough, he was going to leave the toilet that was lower Wacker Drive and walk in the sun again.

But as time passed, and he used the knife he had taken from his attacker more and more, he found that the goal was not foremost in his mind. The cutting was an end in itself.

The first Breather he had operated on had screamed so loudly—eyes rolling to white, spittle foaming at the corners of his mouth—that Grimes had to club him into silence with a plank of wood. In so doing, he had damaged his face. He was useless to him.

So he kept clubbing.

For the second Breather—and the three that followed—he was better prepared. Lower Wacker was filled with pushers and users, so it was not terribly difficult for Grimes to get his hands on some sodium thiopental. A small vial, the liquid as clear as a summer sky. He was also able to secure a vial of chloroform, as well.

That put an end to the screaming. At least until they woke up. Grimes smiled as he thought what that must have been like for these men. Laying their head down for a night's sleep—a brief respite from their monotonous days of hustling in the dark city—only to find upon waking, after emerging groggy and disoriented, not quite certain why they had slept so soundly, that their faces had neatly and primly been removed.

What must their reaction be, Grimes wondered? Their hands would almost certainly go directly to their faces. The pain would not kick in immediately, not until the drugs wore off completely. But there would be a burning sensation and a strangeness that would be impossible to pinpoint. So they would touch their faces and their hands would come away sticky and wet.

Grimes was sure they would scream, staring wide from lidless eye sockets.

He smiled.

At times taking comfort in the pain of others was the only way in which to cope with the fact that, so far, his surgeries were a complete failure. He would suture the flesh from the Breathers over his own raw meaty face, and for a time it would work beautifully. The makeshift surgeries at least allowed him parole from the hell of Lower Wacker. Of course, he commanded many nervous stares while out on the street. That was to be expected, but the streets of any big city such as Chicago were filled to brimming with all sorts of cripples and invalids and the infirm. Victims of a thousand grim abuses, all wearing the scarlet scars of their pain.

So what was one more, Grimes figured.

But by day's end, the skin would slacken. It would hang loose, drooping like melted wax, and then it would slough off entirely, falling to the ground with a splat.

Grimes was determined, however. He would not give up. He would continue to experiment until he got it right.

But now, pushing through the throngs of rush hour commuters swarming home for the evening, Grimes could think of nothing but Verona. Lovely Verona. The mistress who had kept him warm on so many bitter nights, the woman who had simply vanished like smoke when Grimes lost his license to practice medicine.

That was still a tough pill to swallow. He had never thought they were in love. He was not so stupid as to think such a thing. But he did feel that he had at least earned some sense of obligation over the years. There should have been some commitment on her part.

But when the money was gone, so too was she.

Oh, well. At least he had the memories, Grimes thought, smiling. He thought of flesh, again, but not sick, corrupted, blackened flesh. He remembered it as it had been. Verona's flesh. Dark brown, as silky as chocolate, musty and covered by a sheen of slickness. The thought that Grimes could never again enjoy flesh such as that—human contact, skin to skin—was like a needle-jab of pain and regret.

He was dead, yet he was not dead, and although he could relish in the pleasure of splitting flesh away from bone with his knife for as long as it held his interest, he had to accept the fact that the other pleasures of the flesh—those of love and sex—were lost to him forever.

He supposed it was the memory of their nights together, the sweetness of her pink lips, the fullness of her brown thighs, that brought him back to her apartment now. She lived just off the sparkling strand of the Magnificent Mile, in a small brownstone with a black gate in front. Grimes stood in the somber early evening air, staring up at the window of her bedroom. There was no movement inside, at least none that he could see.

But she was here. He was certain.

In the deep pockets of his tan trench coat, Grimes spun the handle of the knife around and around, occasionally pricking the tip of his finger with its sharpness, reveling in the cold blast of pain that shuddered through him. But it was unsatisfying because it was only an imagined pain. It was nothing concrete, nothing firm, for the dead feel no pain.

Sometimes a person needed pain. Grimes had known that all his life, long before his father had clobbered the lesson home for him.

And now Grimes thought that pain would be nice. An interesting diversion.

He opened the gate.

UNDERBELLY.

"THE AIR IS DEAD DOWN HERE," Victor said. "Like a sickness."

It was early morning, just past dawn, yet Lower Wacker was preternaturally dark. Always dark, Jonas thought. Always dark.

Jonas had no idea exactly what to expect as he and Victor descended into the gloom beneath the busy streets of Chicago. Jonas was afraid; that much he knew. Those who dwelled down here sent icy fingers of fear through him. Like his famous companion, they were dead and yet . . . they were not.

And what of his beloved daughter?

What of Jillian?

He could not bear to see her again. The pain in her eyes, the way she looked at Jonas without any sign of recognition. Without any memory of what she had meant to him. How much he loved her.

Jonas and Victor circled through the dank urban gloom, anticipating the ragtag human army that had erected its own city of cardboard, hunched over smoky trash fires. But instead, they found nothing.

"Something's wrong?" Jonas said.

The black-grimed streets were vacant.

Nearby, one of the chain link fences the city had recently erected in the failed hopes of keeping the homeless out of Lower Wacker rattled.

Jonas and Victor turned. Out stepped a lean figure, ragged and dirty, blowing into his pencil thin fingers.

"These are dangerous streets, gentlemen. You of all people should know that, Jonas. Lot of people anxious to drag a knife across your throat."

"What people might that be?" asked Victor. "It would appear there has been an exodus."

Cooper Shaye smiled crookedly, slyly, the corners of his lips curling skyward. "And who might you be?" Shaye jabbed a bony finger toward Jonas. "Him, I know. But you are new around here. And I'll be honest, I am not impressed by the company you keep."

"We're here to help, Shaye," Jonas said.

Shaye's face grew suddenly dark, his gaunt features as stark as a razor's edge. "I warned you. I told you not to head down the dark path that led to Lucias Angel's door. But you did not listen. And so now your daughter is one of us. Confused and afraid and cold, her mind a muddle of memories from a past life that is little more to her than a dream. You have not forgotten how she reacted when she saw you. You are nothing to her now. You are no longer her father. She does not need you. She does not need your help."

"I have traveled a great distance," Victor said coldly. "I would like to see the people Lucias Angel has created. Can you take me to them?"

"Why would I do that? They are not particularly trusting of outsiders."

Victor reached out his right hand, the delicate hand, and took hold of one of Shaye's narrow wrists. Shaye reeled backward, his eyes opening wide. What was it that he was seeing, Jonas wondered. Did he see visions of death? Visions of life?

Victor dropped his hand away; Shaye stood rubbing his wrist, his eyes dark. "You are one of us? One of Angel's forgotten children?"

Victor shook his head. "I fear my solitude has stretched into two centuries. I am no one's child. But neither am I an outsider to these people. Will you take me to them?"

THE HIDDEN.

THE WIND IN CHICAGO HAS TEETH. It lurks around corners, dwells in the darkened alleys between buildings, waiting. And when it pounces, it does so violently, tearing at passersby, ripping at clothing, clawing at exposed flesh, turning it red and raw.

Jonas had never grown accustomed to it. Moving along the sidewalk on LaSalle Street, hugging the western edge of Lincoln Park, Jonas, Victor, and Cooper Shaye made their way slowly north. Jonas shoved his hands into his pockets and hunched his shoulders against the cold.

After a half hour of walking in silence, Shaye dashed across the street, car horns blaring, and cut between two apartment buildings. Jonas and Victor followed.

Shaye moved like an apparition. He would disappear behind a parked car, only to reemerge next to a garbage-streaked dumpster, vanish along the edge of a chain link fence, only to reappear beside a battered mailbox. Jonas lost sight of him innumerable times. He had even considered giving up his pursuit. But Victor never swayed. He followed him doggedly, tracing his footsteps.

And so Jonas continued forward, the wind snapping at him, his lungs burning from the cold. As they cut through a small tree-clustered park, LaSalle Street fell away behind them. Ahead, Jonas could see the gray shimmer of Lake Michigan. A gravel path led them down a sloping hill. At the bottom a stone wall abutted the hill, covered in wriggling ivy. Beneath the green, tangled leaves, Jonas could discern the slightest glint of sunlight off metal. It was a door, almost entirely obscured behind the wild mat of greenery.

Shaye pulled a key from his front pocket and fumbled for a moment with the door, glancing every so often over his shoulder. Finally the door creaked inward, the ivy hanging in cascades over the entrance. Shaye brushed it aside with one lean arm and stepped inside.

Jonas and Victor followed.

"How long have you lived in this city?" Shaye asked Jonas.

"How long? Forever. I mean, all my life."

"Bet you never knew this was here, did ya?"

"Where are we going?"

Shaye smiled. "Do you like animals?"

The door slammed shut behind them and they were thrown into darkness.

"Put your hand out," Shaye said. "Your left hand. Run it along the wall. We'll walk straight ahead, about a hundred yards or so."

The wall was cold to the touch. And covered with a fine sheen of wet filth. But Jonas did as Shaye advised. They walked forward slowly. Blackness pressing in on them.

Twice Jonas moved too fast—he was in a hurry to get out of this passageway—and thumped headlong into Victor's back.

The darkness was almost overwhelming. Jonas's eyes strained for any glint of light, but he could see nothing. Absolutely nothing.

Then there was a chalkboard squeal and a sliver of light spilled out onto the hard concrete floor. Another door.

Shaye disappeared, as did Victor. Jonas followed. He emerged in another narrow passageway, this one illuminated by bare overhead lightbulbs encased in thick wire mesh. Even after so short a time immersed in the darkness, the lights seemed overly bright, like tiny suns dotting the ceiling. The floors were concrete, as were the walls. Above their heads, thick pipes and vents slithered, many of them black with fungus and decay.

"It's best to keep your voices down," Shaye advised. "Sometimes we get surprised in here."

"By what?"

Shaye smiled. "If I told you then it wouldn't be a surprise."

The corridor wound for what Jonas thought must have been another hundred yards before a low, guttural roar shattered the tranquility. Jonas jumped.

"What the hell was that?"

"I think that may have been the surprise," Shaye said.

Shaye grabbed Jonas by the sleeve and directed him toward a small, darkened alcove. Next, he pushed Victor in and then crowded in himself. "Keep quiet. And keep still. It won't be able to smell Victor or me. One of the advantages of being the undead. But you are a different story, Burke. Just flatten yourself against the wall and hold still."

The growling drew closer. Thick and muscular. It sounded monstrous to Jonas, but also very familiar.

"Quiet, Neena. Sshhhh." A male voice commanded.

The growling persisted. Then, a smell. Musty and raw. Jonas flared his nostrils.

He peered over Victor's shoulder, standing on tiptoe. In the harsh light of the corridor, a thin man suddenly came into view. Beside him there stood another man, much thicker and well muscled. They both held a metal pole, which was attached to a rolling cage.

And in the cage . . .

"A lion?" Jonas whispered.

Shaye spun and glared. *Be quiet*, the stare said.

Jonas struggled for a moment with what he had seen. The sight of a lion in the midst of downtown Chicago was so alien to him, so incongruous, that he had trouble believing his own eyes. Then it struck him, suddenly. A sharp flash of insight.

"Lincoln Park Zoo," he whispered.

A strong arm snagged the collar of his coat and pulled him back out into the corridor. He was face to face with Shaye, nearly nose to nose. He could see the hollow scepter of death reflected in the man's eyes. "These tunnels wind for miles. A person could easily get lost in here. Wander for days, disoriented and alone."

Jonas had been a visitor to Lincoln Park Zoo countless times. With Katherine in the years before they were married, then, again, two or three times a year after their daughter's birth. Jillian had loved it. Always. Since the moment she was born.

It was one of Chicago's few remaining attractions that was free of charge to the public. Jonas had always thrilled to the otherworldliness of the zoo, to the strangely surreal feeling of walking through downtown Chicago and then suddenly, by simply going through a small, gated turnstile, coming face to face with elephants, hippos, baboons, jungle cats. It was all so dreamlike. No matter how many times he visited, it always took him a few minutes to grapple with the reality that in the shadows of the city's great sky scrapers, so many of nature's most exotic creatures lived out their days and nights.

It was a fantastic place, unique and magical and Jonas had always felt at home here. But, of course, that was above ground, in the bright sunshine of a warm summer day. He had never been *beneath* the zoo. Had never been in the dark, musty corridors that ran below the cold ground like arteries.

Had never even realized they existed.

"There is a medical lab to care for the sick animals, and a galley where some of the larger animals are bathed, and countless pens," Shaye said. "The zoo is open all year round and many of the animals simply cannot stay above ground without respite from the cold. There are research facilities down here as well, and small apartments for some of the staff. And there are many abandoned areas. Dark, forgotten areas that humans have given up years ago. That is where we have made our home. In the dark places."

Shaye drifted down the corridor, a spectre, as ephemeral as smoke. Gray-white. Victor followed, quietly, head bowed. Jonas stood for a moment in the dank corridor, listening as the now far-off roar of the lion echoed like the lingering memory of a nightmare. Then, he too, followed his two undead companions as they wound deeper and deeper into the waiting darkness.

LAMB TO SLAUGHTER.

THEY WALKED IN SILENCE, hugging the walls as they
went. They passed a small, dimly lit room where a young
man in the brown khaki uniform of the Lincoln Park Zoo
sat behind a desk, shuffling papers.

They passed the animal infirmary, its metal doors
shuttered. They passed another locked door, and then
another.

And then there was only darkness. The corridor
continued on, but the overhead lights did not. The
blackness was complete and overwhelming. Onward they
continued, through corridors as black as the mouth of
Hell, through passageways that had most likely been
neglected since the zoo opened its gates.

Finally, a dim pinprick of light. Mustard yellow, and
weak. It was not far off, less than fifty feet in the distance.

They came upon a ragged opening that had been hacked into the wall, just above eye level. Through it shone the desperate light.

Shaye wriggled through the tight opening, his head, arms, body and finally legs disappearing as if being swallowed. Victor followed.

When all was clear, Jonas gripped the side of the opening, the shattered concrete nipping at the palms of his hands, and pulled himself up. Halfway through, his legs still dangling in the corridor from which they had come, hands were suddenly upon him, pulling, tugging, yanking him into dead air. After a brief moment of panic, Jonas was lowered gently to his feet. Surrounded him, clothes in tatters, faces darkened with soot and soil, were the offspring of Lucias Angel's dark work. There were hundreds of them. Dead, expressionless faces. Black eyes. Staring not so much at Jonas as past him. Through him. As if he were transparent. The invisible man.

The room was dimly illuminated by a lone lightbulb dangling from the high ceiling. Garbage littered the ground, strewn in every direction, packed into the corners, heaped into mounds on the floor. It was dark, so very dark. One weak lightbulb, Jonas thought. That was all that separated everyone in this pitiful room from utter blackness.

Jonas scanned the dim room, moving his gaze from one blank face to another. "Is . . . is she . . .?"

"Yes. She is here. Somewhere. Your voice may have frightened her. I have told you, you are nothing to her. Not even a memory."

"I don't believe that. Somewhere, deep inside, she must remember something. She must remember what she meant to me."

"Don't delude yourself," Shaye said coldly. "You will only cause yourself grief."

Victor fanned out among the living dead, his arms outstretched, Messiah-like, touching the great, unwashed hordes. His dark gray eyes were moist and distant. Jonas knew that only Victor could have walked among them in such a way. Without alarming or disturbing them. Some even approached him, skittish, but curious. He belonged among them. Somehow they all knew that.

"You can't stay here forever," Jonas said to Shaye. "It's miserable down here."

"Yes, it is," Shaye returned, making no attempt to hide his contempt. "But above ground there is so much violence among us. And death. Something bad is happening on Lower Wacker. Bodies of Breathers are turning up, mutilated, their faces torn away. It won't be long before the police come to crack some heads. And I don't want these poor souls to suffer any more."

"Then what do you plan to do? We've come to help. If you will let us."

Shaye smiled. "I cannot decide about you, Jonas Burke. You are either as evil as Angel himself or you redefine the notion of naiveté. We want nothing from you. Even if we did, what is it that you think you would do? We know what lies ahead for us. We know what must be done."

"And what is that?"

Shaye's smile remained. It was a mocking smile, filled with hatred and disdain. "We must seek peace." Then the smile slid from his face, washed away in the blink of an eye, vanished as if he had been offended. "The time will come soon. We shall seek peace and leave the bondage of our bodies behind."

"What are you talking about, Shaye? These people do not know what they are doing. They are . . ."

"Demented? Insane? Feeble?"

"Don't play sanctimonious with me. They have no idea what you will lead them into."

"They will follow, because they trust me. I am the only one. And you should not be one to preach of sanctimony. Do not pretend for a moment that you understand anything these people are going through. You do not. You will not. Not ever. Everything I do is to allow these people to be freed from their pain. What is the shame in that?"

"You still haven't told me what you plan to do."

"I cannot trust you."

"Right now, your choices are limited. Me and Victor are all you have."

"I don't want you."

"What are your plans, Shaye. Tell me. I will not let you hurt my little girl."

A gurgling laughter exploded from Shaye's mouth. "Don't hurt your little girl. My God, why is she here,

Jonas? Who brought his darling little girl to Lucias Angel and offered her up like a sacrificial lamb?"

"She can be saved. All these people can be saved. I know it."

"Is that what Lucias told you as he ushered you out of his office? These people are dead. *Dead.* There is no saving them. No changing what they are. There is only one thing in the world that can alleviate the agony, only one thing that can quell the misery—a baptism of fire. And that is what I intend to provide for them."

"You are going to burn them? Set them afire?"

"It is the only way to destroy the corporeal body and free their souls."

"I won't let you."

"You have no choice. If you doubt me, I can give you a demonstration. One word from me, and this horde will tear you limb from bloody limb. I think you know that I am telling you the truth."

"But why . . .?"

"You cannot understand, Jonas. You cannot know the torture we endure every day."

Jonas rubbed his eyes. Since the day he had first met Lucias Angel he had always held out hope that Jillian could be saved. That she could be brought back to him. That's why he had returned with Victor. There had to be a way, but Shaye was intent to destroy any chance he had of being with his daughter again. Shaye planned to destroy everything.

"When?" Jonas asked.

"There are things to be done first, but it will not be long. We have accomplished our first objective. Now all that remains is to burn Lucias Angel to the ground so that he may not create any more like us."

"First objective? What was that?"

Shaye turned away and reached for something on the ground. A flashlight. He handed it to Jonas. "In the far corner there is an entrance to another room. There is no light. I will come with you. I don't think all these little lost children would like you walking among them. Who knows what might happen."

"What are we going to look at?"

"You asked about our first objective. I am going to show you. Start walking."

Jonas clicked the flashlight to life.

Victor was sitting on the ground, his legs folded underneath him, surrounded by a group of haggard souls, touching him, pulling away, then touching again.

Jonas moved through the thick, gray-black expanse of the room, stepping over prostrate bodies, crippled bodies, writhing on the floor like vermin. A few of them reached out for his ankles, grabbing for him. Hell on earth, Jonas thought, tortured souls clambering over one another, their mouths twisted in silent screams.

Jonas looked over his shoulder to assure himself that Shaye was following. At the back of the room, on the far wall, there was a black hole. A doorway. Jonas poked the beam of the flashlight into the murk. From behind, Shaye nudged him forward.

Jonas lurched into the tiny room. The walls pressed in on him from all sides, vise-like. He struggled for air.

For a moment, Jonas fought the disquieting feeling that he was stepping into a trap.

The room was small. Square. Indistinct. Nothing on the floors. Jonas sighed. "What am I looking for?" he said.

A hand grabbed his wrist. Jonas recoiled from Shaye's frigid touch. Shaye held firm, guiding his arm upward, guiding it slowly, until the flashlight's milky beam came to rest high up on one of the gray concrete walls.

Jonas stifled the urge to scream. He was sure, even though he could not see him, that Cooper Shaye was smiling.

A body, naked and bloody, hung against the wall, railroad spikes driven through the wrists and ankles, a length of chain biting into the corpse's neck. It was a young man, the hair scalped from his head, his fingers and toes all violently removed. Shaye followed Jonas's stare.

"I had to let them have a little fun before we slit his throat," Shaye said. "Ten fingers, and ten toes was a small price to pay for what he had done."

"Who is it? Why?"

Shaye plucked the flashlight from Jonas's numb hand and moved the beam over the body, slowly. "We are not certain of his real name. Owen something. We knew him only as the Bone Welder."

The light came to rest on the corpse's groin. Meaty and streaked with blood, Jonas could see that they had removed more than the man's fingers and toes.

"He was Lucias Angel's right hand man. His doctor, so to speak."

"He was the one who did all the experiments," Jonas said in a near whisper.

Shaye nodded. "The pain he inflicted . . . The joy he derived . . . He did not so much like reanimating whole bodies. That was dull to him. He enjoyed the experiments that involved cutting pieces of flesh away, reattaching dead flesh to dead flesh. Like Baron Frankenstein himself. We were too kind to him. We should have made him suffer more."

"So that leaves Angel."

"Yes, and we must move quickly. It will take him no time at all to find another Bone Welder. The world is filled, I'm afraid, with people who can only derive pleasure out of others' pain."

"And when you are through with Angel, you are going to burn every one of the people down here to ashes?" Jonas looked away from the mutilated body of the Bone Welder, and looked deep into Shaye's dark eyes. "Including my daughter?"

Shaye did not hesitate in his response. "Yes. Including your daughter."

AWAKE.

COUGH.

COUGH.

COUGH.

Lungs like stone. Rasping. Hacking.

Martin had grown so tired of the coughing. Of the dull ache in his chest. The fluid that formed deep in his throat and forced its way into his mouth.

He wanted to die. He longed for it.

He feared nothing.

When he shed these mortal coils, all would not end. Blackness did not await. Instead, eternal light. He would be immortal, untouchable to time's cruel hands.

A god.

But first he had to die.

Nurses attended him around the clock, deep in the subterranean pathways of Arch Angel Enterprises. They did not so much try to cure him, as comfort him. Curing was out of the question. Martin knew that. And so he had turned to Lucias Angel.

He made promises to Martin. Martin smiled. He liked the promises. He liked what Lucias had said to him.

A tightening in his belly. Pain. As intense as fire. Martin screamed. Nurses rushed to his side. Moist, warm wash towels draped his forehead.

Soon.

LONG PAST MIDNIGHT.

VICTOR MOVED THROUGH THE DARK, careful, his eyes adjusted to the gloom. The door to the guest room of Walton Wallace's small apartment was cracked open. Inside, Victor could see the still figure of Jonas Burke, fast asleep.

He gently closed the door.

He moved slowly down the hallway, the hardwood floors protesting quietly beneath his footfalls. He did not want to wake Jonas. What he needed to do now, he must do alone. He did not want to have to explain his intentions.

It was better that he did it this way. In the dead of night. The mortals of the city deep in slumber.

It was two o'clock in the morning. A time for the dead to roam the night. Victor stepped quietly out into the hallway and made his way to the lobby.

The air outside was crisp, brittle, as if you could snap it off in your hands. Victor moved south along Clark Street, past the all-night diners, the quiet, dark cafes, the small theaters. Traffic was light, the typical late-night revelers returning from a night at the tavern. Victor paid them no attention. He kept his eyes focused on the monolithic building that had just come into view in the distance. Arch Angel Enterprises.

The architecture was unmistakable. Gothic and brooding, gargoyles perched atop rainspouts, faux stone turrets silhouetted against the coal-dark sky. It was nearly identical to that of the castle in Bavaria in which Victor's creator had resided: Castle Frankenstein.

A yearning, gnawing feeling took hold of Victor. A vivid remorse. A disquieted longing. He could remember so well those misty days, when he had first opened his eyes upon a world thought dead to him. So cold. So lonely. The torches of the villagers. Pursuing him. Cold. Lonely. The only home he had ever known, a gray, ramshackle castle, a thousand years past its prime, haunted by ghosts of generations of Frankensteins. Men who toyed with life and death. Men who toiled in areas meant only for God.

A flash of lightning turned the night sky blue. Then black. The air grew still. A storm approached.

Victor continued south, his head bent low, the remembered sound of relentless, angry villagers seeking blood, ringing in his ears.

VISITOR.

VICTOR PEERED through one of the locked glass doors leading to Arch Angel's main atrium. The lobby of the building was vast and uninviting. Behind a circular guard station a young man—no more than twenty years old—leafed lazily through a magazine. Victor pounded on the door. The young man leaped from his chair, the magazine spilling from his hands.

"Jesus Christ," Victor could hear the young man scream, even through the glass. The guard fumbled to compose himself—tugged at his tie, straightened his hair, smoothed his uniform's rumpled sleeves—and approached the door.

Victor was sure the man was unaccustomed to receiving visitors at this hour of night. It showed in his face. A thin dollop of sweat formed on his upper lip.

"I'm sorry, sir," he said. "No admittance without an appointment, sir."

"I am here to see Lucias Angel."

The young man laughed. "Sure. Of course. Why don't you come back in the morning and we'll see what we can do."

"I would like to see him now."

The smile faded. "Sir, you cannot walk off the street and speak with Mr. Angel. You'd have a better shot at meeting with the president. Why don't you run along?"

"He will see me."

"Sir, truthfully . . . I haven't had what one would call the greatest day. Step away from the glass or I call the cops."

"Tell him I am here. That is all you have to do. Call him in his penthouse suite, apologize for waking him and tell him Victor is here to see him."

"How would you like a nice, long night in the holding tank over on Cumberland?" the guard said. "A night with the other crazies might do you some good."

Victor leaned in so that his face nearly pressed into the glass of the door. "What would you say if I were to tell you that the only thing separating my hands from your throat is my extreme patience? That I could bring this glass between us crashing down around our eyes in seconds and crush your windpipe with one hand while I use your intercom to call Lucias myself with the other hand? Would you believe me, young man?"

The guard looked into Victor's gray eyes and blanched. Swallowed hard, like glass had formed in the back of his throat.

"Victor?" the guard warbled, his lips drawn into a thin line of fear. "Is that what you said?"

"A long-lost relative."

OLD FRIENDS.

THE PENTHOUSE OF ARCH ANGEL ENTERPRISES occupied the top two floors of the building, stretching a full city block in all four directions. It was opulent beyond anything Victor had ever seen. Chandeliers cut from Swarovski crystals dangled from the ceilings. Persian rugs of red and gold and orange slept atop floors of Brazilian cherry wood. A Monet adorned one wall, a kaleidoscopic explosion of purple and violet that when viewed from a distance was quite clearly the Tower of London.

"Mr. Angel will meet you in the study, sir. May I offer you a drink?"

Victor shook his head.

"Very well," said the dour old manservant. "Follow me then, if it please you, sir."

Victor was led into the two-story library. Leather-bound books lined hundreds of shelves—shelves that wrapped around the room, enclosing it like a cocoon. In one corner, there sat a dark burgundy leather chair, a standing lamp hunkered behind it. A ladder, with rollers at its base, allowed access to a second floor balcony that ran the expanse of the entire room. Thousands and thousands of books. It was Victor's vision of paradise.

"I will leave you, sir, if you require no other assistance. Mr. Angel will be in momentarily. Good evening."

Victor said nothing as the man retired from the room. He was literally struck speechless. Volumes of Robert Louis Stevenson were within fingers touch. A complete set of Dickens, all first editions. Proust and Shakespeare. Steinbeck and Twain. Victor ran his index finger along the spines of the books. Images flashed into his head as his hand alighted each volume. He could see Prospero, thunder rumbling. Huck on the great, rolling river, his smile as wide as the heavens. A broken-down young woman from Steinbeck's dust bowl, near death, mourning the passing of her own baby, suckling a starving man, giving him life.

He saw all these things and more. Then his finger came to rest upon a book slightly larger than the others, its cover blacker than a crow's wings, the leather hard and unforgiving. He pulled the volume from the shelf, slowly, the image of man's fall from grace in the Garden of Eden playing out in his mind's eye.

He turned the book over in his hand. *Paradise Lost*.

"Ah, one of my favorites. The original sin. Been all downhill since." The voice was low and smooth, the sound of brandy being poured. Victor turned toward Lucias Angel.

He wore red silk pajamas under a black silk robe. He was tall, solidly built, shoulders wide and straight. A long mane of dark black hair flowed halfway down his back. He smiled.

Victor grimaced. He was beautiful. Victor had forgotten just how beautiful. For all the ugliness and monstrousness that had been bestowed upon Victor, Lucias Angel looked nothing short of a god. Age-old jealousy worked at him, tugging, needling him. It wasn't fair, Victor told himself, just like he had all those years ago. *It wasn't fair.*

"So tell me, Henry, when did Lucias Angel come into existence?"

Lucias laughed. "I haven't heard that name for a long while. Really, you couldn't expect that I would go through life with the name Henry did you? It is so . . . common. A man such as myself needs a name that reflects his station in life."

"That name seemed to suit you well enough when my father used it to call you his best friend. You remember him, don't you, Henry?"

Lucias waved the question aside. "Have a drink with me, Victor. That is what you call yourself, isn't it? I suppose 'The Monster' did have its limitations."

"We both know *I* am not the monster."

"Some sherry, perhaps. How does that sound? Shall I ring for Jamison?"

"I did not come here for a drink."

Lucias ran his hand along the back of the leather chair. "You came here out of unstoppable curiosity."

"You have something I want."

Lucias laughed, the corners of his smile curling up into soft dimples. His eyes sparkled like diamonds. So damned beautiful, Victor cursed.

"That's funny," Lucias said. "I was about to say the same thing. Do you have it?"

"It won't help you."

Lucias's face hardened. "Do . . . you . . . have . . . it?"

Victor flipped casually through the volume of *Paradise Lost*, the pages supple as velvet. He silently read passages from the epic poem, the words carrying him back to another world, another place. Then he read aloud. "Of that Forbidden Tree, whose mortal taste brought death into the world, and all our woe, with loss of Eden, till one greater Man restore us, and regain the blissful seat."

"You may hold the secret to eternal life, Victor. You *are* aware of that." Lucias's voice was filled with urgency. "You cannot shirk such a responsibility. Cannot run from it. How dare you hide away in the frost and ice with the secrets of eternity at your fingers. So, again, where is it?"

"You of all people should know that I have little interest in eternal life. I do not wish my suffering to be felt by anyone else."

"Oh, are you going to serenade me with your tragic story, Victor. The social outcast, hunted by his fellow man. It's all so sad. Well, spare me the melodrama. I believe Miss Shelley has already provided enough of that."

"Except, as we both know, Henry, she was misinformed about much of what she wrote. She made some very glaring errors."

"The name is Lucias. I am a man accustomed to getting respect, and I have learned ways, over the years, of making certain that I receive that respect. I repeat, the name is Lucias."

Victor snapped closed the volume in his hand and placed it back on the shelf. "I do not have father's journal—his first journal, I should say. Not anymore. And what of the second volume? The one I have never seen?"

Lucias's eyes blackened. "I am afraid the volume you seek is worthless, filled with the ramblings of a mad man. I have used the formulations set forth in its pages and it has yielded me nothing but feeble-minded fools. No, Victor, I am afraid that the information I require is in Dr. Frankenstein's *first* journal, the one he compiled while at University in Ingolstadt. The one you have had in your possession since he spurned you. The one you found in your coat pocket while you were exiled in the woods outside Ingolstadt. I need *that* journal, Victor. Let's not make this unpleasant."

"It has been destroyed. As it should have been. There is but one God, Lucias. Only one creator. What father did was a transgression against nature. It cannot continue."

"Nonsense. He was not defying God's work, he was continuing it. Man was created with a gift that no other creature possesses—that of curiosity, of seeking to know the unknowable. It was God himself who put that yearning in man. Your father's work was but an extension of those great explorers before him—we no longer think of Galileo and da Vinci as heretics, do we? Columbus and da Gama and Cortez are no longer reviled as madmen. Sagan and Einstein and Hawking are not thought of as abstract thinkers, playing games with the cosmos. They all struggled to do just as your father dreamed of doing, of raising man's place in the universe, of understanding that which was once considered beyond man's comprehension. Many mysteries remain—thousands, millions—but one still nags at mankind above all others; the secrets of the grave. The ludicrousness of aging, growing feeble, dying. What is the purpose? What is the meaning? If God created us in his image and expected that we would do his work on earth, then why does he cut our lives short? Why does he murder his own offspring? If God can forever remain immortal, alive as He always has been," he said, "then why too can't His children?"

"Who are you to question God?" Victor asked.

"Who am I that I should *not?*"

Victor turned away. Speaking with Henry—Lucias—was as infuriating as it had been two centuries prior. Victor focused his attention again upon the volumes in the library, the incredible wealth of knowledge and imagination. "A man could become lost in a room such as this."

"A sanctuary. In here, the outside world does not exist. At least not the way it looks to the mortals toiling down below. In here, the outside world exists only having been first distilled through the minds of Bronte and Beckett and Hurston and Woolf."

"I think that I may never leave."

There was a silence then. Both men stared at one another, then at the expanse of books that surrounded them.

Finally, Victor spoke.

"You must stop what you are doing, Henry. And no, I will not call you by any other name. You are Henry to me, a man who meant as much to my father as any man on earth."

"I am so close, Victor. It is within reach. Don't you see?"

"It is a fool's errand."

"Are you suggesting your father, the man who created you from nothing, from dead flesh, was a fool?"

"Alas, yes. A great man, at one time. Certainly he did not intend the evil he unleashed. But a fool nonetheless. Just as I have been. And you, Henry. We have all chased God's secrets and have been punished in kind."

"Victor?"

"Yes, Henry?"

"The loneliness is crippling."

"I know."

"I can stand for it no longer. Others must be created, others like ourselves. The mortals can never understand; their fears and problems and concerns are but nuisances to us. I have had many women. Many. They mean nothing. How can they? They are worried about money, and growing old, and getting wrinkles and keeping their kids neck-high in all the latest fads and gadgets. It's ludicrous. We know there are more important things, don't we."

"You must stop."

"Frankenstein would want us to continue his work. He would want us to solve the puzzle that haunted him to his grave."

"These creatures of yours—they are in pain, Henry. I have seen them. Living like vermin beneath the streets. In darkness and filth."

"That will end. As soon as I perfect my experiments. And you can help. The answer is in that diary. The one you say no longer exists."

"I will not help you. But I'm sure that doesn't come as any great surprise."

"Oh, Victor. You will help me. One way or another. I had hoped that we would work together. But I did not hold out much hope. You were always a bit squeamish on this subject."

A sudden noise startled Victor. He turned just as four men—thickly muscled, scowls dragging their mouths downward—lunged for him. Victor had just enough time to catch a brief glimpse of an opening in one of the bookshelves. A secret compartment. The men crashed down upon him. Victor thrashed and clawed.

Suddenly that horrible feeling was with him again. The feeling of torment, of pursuit, of being an animal meant to be chased, confined and disposed of. Suddenly, these men were no longer lackeys working for Lucias Angel, they were the villagers of Ingolstadt, hounding him, seeking his blood.

He fought hard. One of the men went down and Victor heard a snap. But then more men joined the fray, and then more. Victor was overwhelmed. Panting and exhausted, he was brought to his feet, his arms twisted up stiffly behind his back, four men on either side, pinning him.

Lucias approached, his beatific smile flashing two rows of bright, white teeth. "I told you that you would help me. One way or the other. If you will not tell me what was in Frankenstein's journal, then I will perform my own experiments. You see, Victor, you and I are the only two truly successful resurrections ever performed, if you do not count Christ himself. You out of the parts of the deceased, and myself from a complete corpse. It can be done. We are proof of that. And you, more than even Frankenstein himself, know how to outwit the grave, Victor. After all, you surpassed even the work of your father, or have you forgotten. Surely you remember your own dark experiments. I know that I do. But no matter. If you will not help me then I have no choice but to ascertain how you were created through further experimentation."

Victor stared through heavily-lidded eyes. "Then why not have your flunkies experiment on *you*, Henry. I was a prototype, a dark stab at immortality. But you, Henry. You were the crowning achievement. Isn't that right? You are such a fool."

"Perhaps, but even fools are capable of transcendence. Besides, what choice do you leave me, Victor? It's not as of you are going to divulge how I was reanimated. If you simply revealed that to me, we could end this all right now. The sad reality is that the power to end all these unsuccessful experiments lies with you and you know it. All you would have to do is tell me how I was brought back. But you won't, Victor. That's too dirty for you. Mucking around with mortality. So now who's the fool?"

"What do you plan to do?"

Still smiling. "Your father's work, Victor. Only in reverse. Since you cannot assist me in finding out how you were assembled and sparked to life, then I will disassemble you, piece by piece, to see if I can't discover what makes you tick. You still have a chance to help me. We are family, Victor, and family really shouldn't squabble this way."

Victor spat. "I would rather that I meet you in hell."

"Very well, then. But be forewarned, Victor. I am a man who gets what he wants. That is why I brought you here in the first place."

Victor squinted. "What do you mean, brought me here? I came of my own free will. *I* came to see *you*."

"And you call *me* a fool. You are here because I arranged for it. You were led here like a sheep to slaughter."

Victor thought for moment. *What was Lucias talking about? None of it made any sense. No sense at all . . . unless . . .*

"Jonas," he whispered.

"Mankind has not changed much in all the years you've kept yourself secluded from the world," Lucias said. "Still as duplicitous as ever, I'm afraid. Mr. Burke was in my employ, given the task of luring you from your hideaway in the ice. Does that change anything for you? Maybe provide for a change of heart? You have always wanted nothing more than to belong in this world, Victor. But that is not enough. We should strive to do more than simply fit into this world. We should rule it. Side by side."

Victor said nothing. He could not believe he had been so gullible. He had never experienced anything but pain and humiliation at the hands of the living. Why did he expect that Jonas Burke would have been any different? He stared at Lucias, and still said nothing.

"Very well," Lucias said. "I am sorry." And for but the briefest of moments, Victor thought that he may have been sincere.

"Gentleman," Lucias said, turning to the dozen or so men surrounding Victor, "Tell our new Bone Welder that we have The Monster himself in our grasp."

"Anything else we should tell him, sir?" one of the thick-necked men asked.

"Yes," replied Lucias. "There is. Tell him to prepare for dissection."

LAKESIDE.

IT WAS IMPORTANT, Cooper Shaye decided, to at least *pretend* he was alive. And the others, as well. The Hidden, as he had come to refer to them. They were so emotionally and mentally fragile to begin with, he could see no good coming from locking themselves away in total darkness for now and ever more. They had to get out. Above ground. Smell the fresh air. Feel the sun upon them. Watch the distant blue waters of Lake Michigan lap against the shore.

It was cold, bitterly, yet Grant Park was no less beautiful. Buckingham Fountain, the park's centerpiece, was dormant now, not to be turned on by the city until Memorial Day. Shaye and the other refuse cast aside by Lucias Angel sat in the cold shadow of the fountain, facing east, toward the frigid lake. White caps rolled low on the horizon. Sea gulls bantered to one another, floating like paper planes in the wind.

Cooper Shaye watched the rough waters, reveling in their dark beauty.

"Pretty," Lester Pines said beside him.

Shaye nodded.

"No boats."

"Too rough," Shaye said.

Lester Pines was new to their group, one of Angel's most recent experiments. He, like the others, was deemed an abject failure. Feeble-minded and disoriented. Lost inside a dead body.

"Birds pretty."

Shaye said nothing. This was not a responsibility he wanted. That of babysitter. Of provider. Protector. He wanted none of it. But he knew he had no choice. None of them could fend for themselves. Who knows what might have become of them if he were not there to protect them. And no matter how defiant and strong he sounded when he explained his plans to Jonas Burke, he still could not deny the crushing guilt that overwhelmed him at times.

What gave him the right to extinguish these people forever? Any more than Lucias Angel had the right to curse them with immortality in the first place?

He looked out over their faces now—sunken cheeks, hollow eyes, fear, sadness—and he wondered if any of them had any idea what was in store for them. And if they did, would they even care.

Cooper Shaye shook his head. He didn't want the responsibility—he *resented* it.

But there was no one else.

"Cold water. Wind. Cold," Lester said.

"Yes," Shaye said in return.

Many of the other Hidden were now milling around the fountain, running their hands along the cold brass guardrails, kicking up copper plumes of grit from the pebbled path that encircled it. He would have to round them up soon. It was important that they not stay out too long. Too many bad things could happen.

To the north, Cooper could see Navy Pier, its huge Ferris wheel in relief against the gray sky. He had been there many times before. Had ridden the Ferris wheel. Many times. Long ago.

Suddenly, Olive Grollman was beside him, tugging the sleeve of his coat. "Water?" she asked.

Cooper feigned a smile. "Yes," he said, pointing out toward the lake, "water."

Olive frowned. "No. Water?" And now she was pointing, only in the other direction. Toward the fountain.

"Oh, no," Cooper said. "Not now. In a while. A few months."

"Few months?"

"In a little while, Olive. They'll turn the water on in a little while."

Dissatisfied with the answer, Olive shuffled back toward Buckingham Fountain.

Shaye pulled himself from the ground and made his way into Grant Park. It was deserted, too cold for the multitudes that would crowd here in the summer. He could see the bandshell in the distance where he had seen bands play at the Taste of Chicago and Blues Fest. On the opposite side of the park he could see the Torco building stabbing the sky. His heart sank. It was in that building, many years ago, while attending college, that he had met Jennifer.

Shaye pounded his fists into the side of his head. *Stop it*, he screamed. *Can't take these memories. Don't want them in my head. Too much pain.*

But the memories would never go away; Cooper Shaye knew that all too well. And it was at times like this—when he could picture Jennifer's smile and could clearly see the tears in her eyes the night she had said yes to him—that he envied the others. They had memories of nothing. Nothing. They were not haunted by the ghosts of their past.

Shaye clapped his hands. "Follow me, everyone." No one argued. They simply lowered their heads and made their way toward him, bedraggled. Shaye headed north.

He hesitated and then glanced one last time back at the Torco building. They sat in circles on the floor in the hallways, so long ago, telling stories, laughing. Then one day, Jennifer had touched his hand.

Turn away, he told himself. *Turn away.*

But he did not. Because something had caught his eye. Some movement. A flash of activity at the far end of the park. He squinted. It was . . .

"Oh, no," he said, quietly.

He turned and looked over the legions of the dead whom had become, in absentia, his children. He scanned quickly, face to face to face. He did not see her.

He turned his attention back to the far end of the park— so far away. It was *her*. He was sure of it.

Jillian. The pretty one. And there was someone with her. A man. He was leading her away, glancing furtively over his shoulder.

"Dammit," Cooper Shaye cursed. They were too far away, and he was helpless to come to her rescue. The man turned toward Shaye, but Shaye already knew his identity. Of course he did. Cooper Shaye only knew of one man fool enough to do something like this.

"Burke," he yelled. "Come back here. What do you expect to do with her? She's ours now. Ours."

Jonas Burke did not stop nor did he look back again, not even for a second. He grabbed his daughter by the arm and pulled her across Michigan Avenue, busy as ever, horns blaring, tires screeching. He half-galloped, Jillian trying to keep pace, stumbling, and then they both disappeared into the steel and glass jungle of skyscrapers that comprised Chicago's Loop. Vanished.

Gone.

Cooper Shaye sighed.

REMEMBRANCE.

MARTIN AWOKE as if from a dream. Only it had not been a dream. He had been dead. And now . . .

What?

He was not alive. Not among the living, that would be impossible. But neither was he dead for he could see and hear and speak. He was neither, he supposed.

He was the *un*dead.

He felt no pain. In fact, he felt . . . nothing. He was neither hot nor cold, calm nor anxious. It was as if he were floating above the earth, ever so slightly, his feet hovering inches from the ground. He moved slowly, awkwardly. At first, every step took a concerted effort. Like a paraplegic learning to walk again. He was stiff and uncoordinated.

Now he moved with ease.

He had no urges nor desires. He did not think of sex nor of food nor of drink. Those desires were all for the corporeal flesh. They were the chains that bound mankind to subservience to his basest instincts. Martin was free from those.

Free.

Suddenly, a voice.

"Are you . . . okay?"

Martin blinked, the room around him shifting hazily into view. Blinked again.

"What? Yes. Fine."

A flurry of activity. People—a great many of them—scattered as if a gunshot had gone off. There was a frenzied excitement. And it was clear to Martin, although he was not sure why, that he was the reason.

"Simmons, he's awake," someone shouted, their voice hoarse and shrill. "Clear-eyed. Composed. I think you should come here."

And then Simmons was beside Martin. Smiles. Twinkle in his eyes. Martin had no idea why the man seemed so happy.

"Do you know where you are?" Simmons's voice was like poured syrup. Slow and soothing.

Martin nodded. He did not know his exact location, not the specific room. But he knew he was still in the basement of Arch Angel Enterprises. The walls in the room were nondescript, plain cinder block. But he could tell instantly that it was not the room in which he had been harbored before his death. It was much more sterile. Empty and cold.

"You've moved me," Martin said. "But only to a different room. We're still in the same building."

"How do you know that?" Simmons asked, his voice pouring over Martin.

"I can't explain. Just something you can feel in your bones. They way the air moves, the smell."

"You are very perceptive." Simmons smiled like a proud father staring through the glass of the maternity ward.

Despite his best intentions, Martin scowled. "Excuse me . . . but, why are you speaking to me like that?"

"Like . . . what?"

"That," Martin snapped. "Like I am a preschooler. Is there something wrong?"

Simmons smiled wider. "Forgive me," he said, "I did not mean to offend. But I wonder if you would be terribly inconvenienced if I were to ask you a few simple questions?"

"Don't see any harm."

"All right then. Be forewarned that many of these questions may seem rather elementary, but they are important to ask nonetheless."

Martin nodded.

"Do you know what day it is today?"

Martin thought for a moment. Monday? No, Thursday. He realized that he had no way of knowing. Fever had grasped him on the 22nd, a Wednesday. Then, the chills had followed. Delirium. And then . . .

"No," he replied. "Not exactly."

"That's fine. Nothing to worry about. How about where you are, do you know that?"

"The basement of the Ar . . ."

"I apologize. Forgive me. I meant the city that we are in."

"Chicago," Martin said quickly.

"Are you certain?" Smiling. Always smiling.

"Unless you've moved the building."

Simmons laughed, and it did not seem canned or fake. And although Martin knew that what he said was not even remotely humorous, the man was finding great joy in it.

"You like Chicago, don't you? When did you move here? Do you remember that?"

Martin pulled his eyebrows together. How many years had it been? "Twenty," he said. "No, I'm sorry. Twenty-one. Moved here from Mayfield, Nebraska, of all places. This city seemed as big as the whole world when I first moved. Still does sometimes, I guess."

Simmons was now looking around the room, at the other people who stood in a semicircle around he and Martin. His smile said a great many things to these people, all of whom smiled back.

"Is it okay if I ask what the hell is going on around here?" Martin said. "Either that or give me one of the happy pills you've all been taking."

Now there was laughter throughout the room, echoing off the pale cinder-block walls like cannon shot.

"Everything will be clear to you soon, Martin. You have nothing to worry about. I must ask you . . . no headaches? No disorientation?"

Martin nodded.

"It's perfectly normal if there is," Simmons reassured.

"No, really. I feel quite good. Powerful. More so than ever before in my life."

Smiling. "Tremendous. And your thoughts? They are clear? No problem with memory? Like for instance the high school you attended?"

"South Hampton. Graduated with honors."

Smiling. "And how about college?"

"Boston University. Did not graduate with honors."

Smiling. "That's a good school. Very good indeed. What was your favorite subject?"

"I don't know. History, I suppose. Liked science, too."

Smiling. "Me, too. Especially science. I have often dreamed of traveling to the stars. How about you, Martin?"

"Of course. Seems a far off dream now. As a kid I would stare up at the night sky and think about walking across the face of the moon. Setting up camp in the Sea of Tranquility. And, then there was Mars, red as fire, shining like a beacon. For some reason I was obsessed with Olympus Mons, couldn't tell you why?"

Then another voice, not Simmons'. "Olympus Mons?" It was a short woman, fair complexion, eyes as round as walnuts. Simmons still smiled.

"The largest mountain range in the solar system," Martin said. "Four times the height of Everest. Can you imagine? I would dream of climbing it. Hell, just of seeing it. How amazing that would be . . ." Martin stopped himself short, suddenly feeling ridiculous in the midst of this reverie in front of a room full of strangers.

There was complete silence. They all stared, slack-jawed. Martin felt like a museum piece, a specimen in a zoo. What is wrong, he wanted to ask. Was just about to ask when Simmons, smiling, smiling, smiling, spoke, the words trickling out like warm rain. "We have done it, people. Finally. Finally. Mankind has reached a new apex, another step forward in our evolution. We have done it."

And then there was cheering. Martin, dumfounded, could think of nothing else to do but return everyone's smiles.

REUNION.

IT WAS NOT THE COLD ITSELF that disturbed Cooper Shaye, but rather the *lack* of effect it had upon him that left him in a cloud of longing and depression. Like so many things — hunger, sexual desire, sleep — his reaction to Chicago's biting weather had fallen away from him. Sloughed off like the skin of a molting snake.

As he walked along Michigan Avenue, he watched the Breathers rush past, coats, gloves, scarves, hats, plumes of white mist blasting from their mouths. They shivered. They grimaced, teeth clenched.

Yet, Shaye felt nothing.

He strolled slowly, hands in pockets, staring into the bright boutiques and coffee houses along the way. It was early morning, the sky as gray as gun metal. Breathers pushed past him, shopping bags in hand, clogging the sidewalks and intersections.

At Water Tower Place Cooper Shaye stopped. It was a great, square, white and gray marbled building that stood on the tip of Chicago's Magnificent Mile, the crown jewel of the city's most luxurious shopping district.

Suddenly there was a pain in his chest. A dull ache. When Cooper Shaye at last realized what it was, he was grateful that not every one of his basic human desires had been erased by the grave. Food, drink and sleep may mean nothing to him now, but the longing of companionship remained. The touch of another.

The love he felt for his wife.

He and Jennifer had been here many times together. As a publisher, Shaye did not make the kind of money that would allow him to shop here often, but he and Jennifer had always enjoyed window shopping. Had enjoyed the wide-eyed crowds.

Cooper shut his eyes, and for a moment he could see her. Brown hair falling to the middle of her back, crooked smile. That's how she had looked when they met. Then the kids had come, and she had cut the hair short. She spun in front of him, dancing in the wistful darkness of his mind's eye. She smiled her crooked smile.

He opened his eyes.

But she was still there.

Cooper Shaye blinked.

Jennifer was still in front of him.

Waiting in line for the 53 bus, a bag from Crate & Barrel in her right hand.

Shaye closed his eyes. Hard. He was seeing things. He so missed her that he had conjured an image of her—not only in his mind—but also on the street right in front of him. People nudged him as he stood silently, eyes closed. Some cursed under their breath.

She is not here, he told himself. *The mind does things like this; creates fantasies to ease pain. She is not here.*

He opened his eyes. Jennifer stood, just as she had for the past few minutes, shifting on her heels, checking her watch.

"Oh my God," Cooper whispered. Then louder, "Oh my God."

He lurched forward, unthinking. Acting on impulse. To touch her again. To feel her warmth against his body.

To see her smile.

He pushed past the throngs of shoppers, sightseers, tourists. Her hair had grown out again. It was past her shoulders, tied into a ponytail. Her skin was as white and flawless as he remembered.

Now if only he could see her smile. If only . . .

She looked up.

Her reaction was slow to build. Her eyes narrowed, and she appeared to have lost her breath. Then she took a step back. Right off the curb and into the busy street. Cars began to honk. From his window, a bus driver screamed for her to move.

Again, Cooper reacted out of instinct. He charged for her. She was in danger. He had to protect her.

Then the screaming began.

Jennifer's mouth widened; her hands shot to her face. And she screamed.

"Honey, no, no, it's okay," Cooper said, coming toward her.

Her hands began to tremble and she began to swoon, as if she were going to pass out. Cooper pressed forward. Still concerned for her. Still worried that she could be injured. The bleating of horns grew louder.

"It's me. It's Coop . . ."

"No," she screamed. A young man, also waiting on line for the bus, went to her aid, grabbing her by the elbow, steadying her. His eyes came up to meet Cooper's and they were black with fear and hatred.

"What are you doing, man?" the young man said. "Get away from her."

"But . . ." Cooper began to plea. Then he saw the eyes of the other surrounding strangers begin to turn toward him. "I'm . . ." *I'm her husband, he wanted to say. Cooper Shaye. She is Jennifer Shaye. We were married on the island of St. Thomas, nine years ago. We have two young children. Benjamin and Lilly. The loves of my life.*

That's what he wanted to say.

But the crowd was now starting to close in around him. He could smell the anger. Like a black cloud.

"Leave her alone."

"Get the hell outta here."

"It's okay, ma'am, we'll take care of this guy."

Hateful stares. The bodies pressed in around him. A vise made of living flesh.

"You sonuvabitch. You coulda killed her."

Jennifer was back on the sidewalk now, but the screaming continued, grew louder. She fell to the ground, began convulsing.

Jesus Christ, Cooper thought. *What have I done? You fool. She buried you. Or at least she thought she did. She had no way of knowing the black plans Lucias Angel had for you. How easy it was to simply switch the bodies. She knows none of that. All she knows is that she mourned you and cried for you and buried you in the ground more than two years ago and now you show up on the street, running toward her, calling for her. What was I thinking?*

A group had gathered around Jennifer. They rubbed her forehead. In the distance, Cooper could hear the razor-edged wail of squad cars arriving.

He pushed through the crowd. Pushed. Pushed. Hands grabbed for him. But Cooper could not be brought in by the police. How could he possibly explain all that had happened to him? How could he possibly . . .?

He raised his forearm and charged. The pedestrians, the angry mob, parted. They wanted to help the young lady whom they perceived to be in danger, but they also did not want to endanger themselves. Cooper ran as fast as he could toward the lake and then cut south along the neighborhood side streets.

He ran and ran.

All the time, the image of his wife in his head. How beautiful she looked until her mouth had curled into a grimace and she began to scream, scream at the sight of her long-dead husband.

THE GOOD DOCTOR.

SCREAMS WRENCHED THE STAGNANT AIR of the house like razor blades tearing through black fabric. Howls of pain. Of loss. Of desire. Of need.

On the west side of the city, there were more of these unfortunate houses than anyone dared admit. Houses where the destitute and lost came to escape their pain, only to unearth greater suffering than they could have imagined.

They all looked the same. Battered and weary on the outside. Paint chipping. Porch slanting into the brown lawn. Awnings orange with rust. The glass of the barred windows bashed out, pieces of torn cardboard in its place.

On the inside, worse. Dark. Stagnant. Reeking of unwashed bodies, vomit, urine, semen. A waking nightmare. Darker than Hades. No escape.

A crack house.

In the basement, strapped to a gurney with steel-reinforced bands around wrists and ankles, Victor could hear the screams, could feel the despair and terror. Victor was a captive, secreted away to this haunted place against his will. But the people upstairs—blank-eyed, sunken cheeked, skeletal and frail—they came here of their own free will. They chose to be here. How could that be? Victor wondered. No one volunteered to enter hell. No one except the devil himself. What could make people want this for themselves?

Victor closed his eyes, and for a moment the screams he heard were not those of others; they were his own. The screams of electricity, of needles stitching together violated flesh. The screams of his own birth.

His eyes snapped open, and he again surveyed his gray, dismal surroundings. Concrete walls, concrete floors. A row of three overhead lights, encased in darkened plastic covers, that twisted light into aberrations, casting shadows where shadows should not have been. Next to him, strapped to another gurney, a middle-aged man, bearded, mouth agape, both arms removed above the elbows, blood fanning out beneath the open wounds.

The man had been screaming when Victor was first brought here. High-pitched, ragged with pain and fear. Then the screaming disintegrated as his voice gave way, reducing the suffering man to whispering to himself, mumbled and incoherent, as if speaking in tongues. Finally, his head lulling down to his chest, he fell silent forever.

Victor sighed.

"So it's you," a voice said. Then a man appeared. Short, with wiry hair and eyeglasses that covered nearly his entire puggish face. "It's really you."

He circled the gurney several times, a manufactured smile stretched across his face. Staring.

"Are the stories true?" the man said.

"No stories are ever true," Victor replied.

The man erupted in laughter. "I heard you were cryptic. You don't disappoint. I suppose that's to be expected. You are a bit of a . . . how should I say . . . legend, I suppose."

"My creator is a legend. I am just a throwaway."

"Oh, you are too modest. And I must say that your characterization over the years has been quite unfair in its presentation of your physical qualities. A few scars here and there, to be certain, and the mismatched hands, that's a bit of a shame, but other than that . . ."

"Other than that I'm like any other member of society."

"Not exactly. But neither are you a monster, pardon me for saying so."

"Not all monsters are distinguishable by their outward appearance. There are spiritual monsters, as well. They are the most dangerous."

"Is that what you think of us, Victor? Monsters?"

The man stopped pacing long enough for Victor to look into his green eyes, bright but a bit muddled, like bargain basement emeralds.

"What you do here is sacrilege. You are not men of science. You are ghouls."

The man erupted again. His face reddening as he brought himself under control. "Jesus, Victor. That's a good one. Look at you. An immortal forged from the bodies of the dead and you speak to me of sacrilege?"

"I am not immortal."

"It's been nearly two hundred years. Maybe you lost track in the Arctic. If that does not make you an immortal . . ."

"I survive because I have chosen to do so."

"Really?" The man appeared genuinely surprised. "If I may be so bold . . . You're existence, it could not have been a happy nor pleasant one all these years . . ."

"And so why did I not put an end to my suffering? A permanent end?"

"I mean no offense."

Victor turned his gaze away from the man. He did not want to look at his spider eyes anymore, his hollow grin. "You would not understand."

Still the man circled. Shark-like, unable to stop, unable to remain motionless. "I don't want to hurt you," he said flatly.

"You cannot hurt me," Victor said.

"Surely you feel pain."

"Do whatever it is your master requests."

"Mr. Angel is doing incredible work here, Victor. Incredible. He is not transgressing God; he is continuing in his footsteps."

"God does not need his help."

There was a sudden uproar behind Victor, a rush of excited voices. "Dr. Page," a voice yelled.

Then another, "He is awake."

Then another, "And cognizant."

"What are you talking about," the man, Dr. Page, asked. "What is all the commotion?"

"Martin," someone said.

Suddenly Page's eyes appeared a shade greener, like a bolt of sunlight had passed across his face. "He's cognizant? Is that what you said?"

"Yes, sir."

"Wide awake."

"Smiling."

"Talking."

"Fully cognizant."

"We've turned the tide."

"Yes, sir."

And then Dr. Page rushed from the room, the voices trailing off into silence behind him.

Victor looked over at the violated body of the corpse beside him and wondered how long exactly the man would remain dead.

SCALPELS.

VICTOR WATCHED AS THE SPIDER-LIKE MAN crawled around him, pacing, frowning, scratching his chin, straightening his round glasses.

"I'm sorry," Victor said.

"You're sorry?" Page huffed, his insect eyes small and cold. "What are you sorry about?"

"For whatever it is that happened after you last left me. You were euphoric. And now . . ."

"And now what?"

"Now you are not."

Dr. Page reached for a gleaming scalpel, which was laid out neatly, along with a number of other gleaming instruments, atop a stainless steel tray table next to Victor. "Tell me if this hurts," he said. The scalpel sliced neatly into Victor's left leg, just below the knee. Victor watched Page's face for any sign that what he was doing may be disturbing or repulsive to him. His face remained without expression. Just a pinched mouth, pinched eyes, wrinkled forehead, eyes like those of a fly.

"I asked if that hurt."

"Were you hoping that it would?"

A shrill, metallic clang echoed in the thick air of the room. "Goddamn it. This does not have to be unpleasant for you. It doesn't have to be." Page stood for a moment, at the foot of the table, shaking. He removed his glasses and rubbed his eyes. "Is that what you want?"

"I want you to release me from these restraints."

"Stop playing games with me. Stop. I . . . I just didn't want there to be too much pain. That's all."

"Why do humans always assume there is no way around pain?"

"Because sometimes there isn't."

"Then why try?" Victor said.

Page stuffed his glasses in his shirt pocket.

"There will be nothing left of you. They will leave you in pieces."

Victor watched the little man, twitching like a bug, his lab coat swooping out behind him like wings.

"And you think that will teach you something? You think disassembling me—as if I were some type of machine—you think that will yield the secret of life for you?"

Page sighed. "We have no other choice. Every other avenue has been closed to us. Every experiment a failure."

"But earlier . . . your assistants . . . they seemed so excited . . ."

"He failed," Page snapped. "Just like the others. Martin, I think his name was. He was cognizant when he awoke . . . but quickly deteriorated. Now he is like the other refuse this building has spit out onto the street."

Page rubbed his beetle eyes. Then placed his glasses back on the end of his nose. Outside, in the hallway, there was a sudden cacophony of noise. Loud screaming. Glass breaking.

Page sighed. "That will be him."

"Who?" Victor said, quietly.

"The Bone Welder."

"A new one, I presume. The last one did not fare so well."

"Yes, I'm afraid the patients here did not take to him. This one . . . well, you shall see."

The door behind Victor opened. Squealed inward, nails on a chalkboard. Then footsteps. He could feel the man's presence. Could sense him just behind his shoulder. Victor tugged at his constraints, but they would not budge.

Then a face appeared in his line of vision. A twisted mass of flesh. Thick, clotted blood hanging from the man's lips and cheeks and under his blackened eyes. Victor thought the man may have been smiling, but he could not tell for certain. Grizzled strips of flesh dangled down past his mouth.

"Are you ready for me, Frankenstein?" the man said. "I'm ready for you." He produced a gleaming, foot-long steel blade and held it briefly to the light. Turned it slowly. "I suppose I should introduce myself. My name is Doctor

Raymond Grimes. The Bone Welder. Please let me know if I cause you any discomfort."

Then he laughed.

NOT FADE AWAY.

HE HAD BEEN YOUNG. That much he could remember. Not yet thirty, maybe even younger than that.

But there had been an accident. A thunderous crash and then glass falling down around him like rain. Screaming. His own.

There was a man then. When the blackness faded. He promised him things. Wonderful things.

But that was all lost to him now. Everything was enshrouded in a mist of half-memories.

He picked up a piece of glass from the street, a small shard. He turned it over in his hands, sunlight winking.

He stared at his reflection. The contours of his face distorted in the glass. He had not even remembered what he looked like. He squinted. Then shifted his head slowly. His reflection did the same, in reverse.

If only he could remember. Anything. His life. His family. Anything.

But it was no use. His mind was as distorted and fractured as the piece of glass in his hand.

When the thin man came to him and said he would help care for him, he went with him willingly. He told him his name was Cooper.

There were more like him out on these streets. Lost. Brains addled and confused. He was so frightened, but Cooper made him feel a little more whole. Like he was not completely cast out from the world.

Cooper spoke with him, patiently waiting for each slow reply. He wanted to know if he could remember anything but he could not.

He could remember nothing. Only his name.

Martin.

DEEP CUTS.

THE PAIN WAS SHARP AND BITTER. But Victor did not scream, did not so much as flinch. He would not give the Bone Welder the satisfaction.

Grimes began with small incisions on Victor's right forearm. Thin, straight cuts into the flesh that drew no blood. Grimes peeled the skin back, held it open with cold, steel clamps, and probed. Prodded. Trying anything within his power to get a reaction.

Victor fought the animal urge to wince, to bite his lip. He knew this was only spurring Grimes on. That Victor's refusal to whimper and beg was only angering the Bone Welder. But Victor had known this type of man before. Long ago, hounding him with torches and pitchforks, crying for his death.

They were men who screamed for blood, but were never satisfied. It was a bloodlust that could not be quenched.

The Bone Welder cut deeper.

Victor looked down. Could see the tendons of his arm, white and marbled, spilling out onto the table, nearly a dozen gleaming clamps now in place.

"No blood," Grimes muttered, disappointed. The Bone Welder paused, wiped the sweat on his forehead with the back of his hand.

Then, a noise. Bone-chattering, like the monstrous whine of a dental drill. Grimes held the bone saw inches from Victor's face. Smiled. "Now this is going to sting a little," he said.

SPIDER'S WEB.

HOURS HAD PASSED and Grimes still had not returned. The pain, at first excruciating, had settled into a dull throb. But still painful. So very painful.

Victor turned his head, still reeling with the otherworldly feeling, the surreal nausea, that flooded him each time he looked over at the raw stump where his right arm used to be.

Even stranger, more disquieting, was that the arm was still there, on a metal tray just a few feet away, a lifeless piece of meat.

Victor knew that the Bone Welder was only warming up. The lust for pain had grown, darkening behind his eyes.

He would be back soon. And when he did, he would be ready to get to work again. On Victor's flesh. With scalpels and bone saws. And a smile.

But in Victor's mind, it did not matter. To Victor, he had already won the battle and the war. Grimes had given him his best and Victor had stood his ground.

He had not screamed.

"Dear God. What has he done?" Page's face was sour, mouth pinched tightly. He looked first at the ragged wound just below Victor's right shoulder, then turned to the amputated arm. "Christ," Page huffed.

"I thought you would be pleased," Victor said.

"This is not science. You were right about that. There is no method to what he is doing. Just madness. It's . . . barbarism. That's all. Brutality for the sake of brutality."

"Think you could have mutilated me more satisfactorily?"

"Bullshit," Page yelped. "I won't listen to that. I told you what was going to happen. I told you what they would do."

"And yet," said Victor dryly, "you did nothing to stop them."

Page stood motionless for a moment, hands twitching at his side. Such a nervous man, Victor thought. Victor marveled at how Page still appeared to be in motion even when standing still.

A shrill, metallic clattering let Victor know that Page was ready to resume work, that he was pulling another of the gleaming medical instruments from the silver table beside him. What would it be this time, Victor wondered. In his mind's eye he could already feel the rattle of the bone saw cutting through him, the tissue forceps flaying his flesh bare. He braced himself for what was to come.

It wasn't until he felt the tugging at his right shoulder, strong but without the nihilist urgency Victor had experienced with Grimes, that he realized what Page was doing.

"This little attempt at redemption is not going to make the Bone Welder happy," Victor said.

"I'm certain, in the long run, it will make little difference," Page said quietly, carefully pulling the sutures tighter as he began the delicate process of reattaching Victor's right arm. His fingers moved much like the rest of his body, spastically, but with unusual control, like a spider making its way across a web.

"He'll return soon," Page continued. "And I'm afraid he'll finish what he's started."

FOOTSTEPS.

VICTOR LAY FOR HOURS. No longer did he know whether it was morning or night. Light or dark. His back to the door, the room empty save himself, he had little to do but stare at the wall.

And wait.

Twice the door behind him rattled open. Then the clicking of footsteps. He bristled, awaiting the cold caress of steel. But the footsteps receded, the door slammed closed, and he was alone again.

He was not afraid. He was sure Grimes was stalling, taking his sweet time, in the hopes of driving Victor mad with anticipation and worry. But Grimes, connoisseur of pain that he was, had no idea of the torture Victor had already endured. Loneliness. Unbearable solitude. Pain beyond description.

Victor had seen the worst man had to offer and there was nothing Raymond Grimes could do to deepen his resentment.

And yet . . .

This was not how Victor wanted it to end. He'd had very little control over most of the events that had transpired around him since Frankenstein performed his black science; he truly hoped that his "death" would be one of them. No matter, the primal urge to survive was as strong as time itself.

Victor had survived depravity more severe than anything Dr. Raymond Grimes could bring to bear. And somehow—somehow!—he would survive this. He was not about to lose a battle of wills to this man.

Click.

The door swung open. Victor heard it, gentle as it was. He had long since given up trying to strain his neck. He knew it would do no good. He could see nothing.

Footsteps.

Padding toward him. Softly . . .

Victor thought of the blade, the sharp, razor-hewed scalpel as it cut into him, peeling away his flesh. The burring of the bone saw rang in his ears.

The footsteps grew silent.

Silent.

silent

Then hands, thin and strong, reached up from behind the gurney and began to fumble with the leather restraints around Victor's wrist.

Victor bristled. Now what kind of game was Grimes playing? Victor tensed his arm. And waited.

Whatever it was Grimes had planned for him, Victor planned to make him pay dearly for it.

The restraint slid aside. Victor caught a flash of movement beside him. Then he lunged.

His hand wrapped around his captors' neck, tight, and squeezed. Now, for the first time since coming here, Victor screamed.

"You enjoy pain," he said. "Then pain is what you shall get."

Victor allowed all the rage of a lifetime to surge through him. He did not stop when the gurgling reached his ears. Nor when he felt the body begin to sag beneath his steely grip.

He didn't hesitate, not at all . . . until he realized that the man he was choking was not Raymond Grimes, the Bone Welder.

It was Jonas Burke.

PROPHET OF THE DEAD.

"GIVE ME ONE GOOD REASON why I shouldn't kill you," Cooper Shaye growled.

Jonas rubbed his throat, red and raw. It had been nearly as difficult to break away from Shaye's grip as it had been from Victor's. "I thought Jillian and I . . . I thought we could be together again . . . but . . . ," Jonas sighed. Deeply. ". . . she is lost to me . . . forever. Now I know."

The walking dead milled around Jonas, stumbling past, bumping into him, pressing their cold flesh against his. He was back below ground, in the dark caverns beneath Lincoln Park Zoo, the stench of the undead cloying and thick.

Jonas could not bear to admit to Cooper Shaye what everyone already knew: That he had been a fool. Someone once said, although Jonas could not recall who, that every life, when examined by the person living it, seemed a failure. Yet, Jonas had never felt that way. Not entirely, anyway. He was deeply, madly in love with his wife. He was deeply, madly in love with his daughter. He had loved his life.

So much so that all he ever wanted was to get it back.

But sometimes . . .

. . . sometimes it's too late.

Across the shadow-heavy room, he could see her. His baby. Only she was not his baby anymore. Not now. She belonged somewhere else. Her eyes hollow and sad. His Jillian. Jonas cursed himself for having been so stupid.

"Did you think she would remember you? That her mind would return to her, intact and full of fond remembrance?" Shaye looked at him through his steely eyes. Narrow and spiteful.

"I wanted my daughter back, Shaye. I was foolish. But no one, including you, can condemn my motives."

The steeliness, the distant cool anger that nestled in Shaye's eyes like a thorn, was suddenly gone. Replaced by . . . what? Jonas could not tell for certain, but it was clear his words had struck a chord with him. Perhaps Shaye was thinking about his own loved ones. Those he had left behind and would never see again.

Jonas watched for a moment. The dead. Shuffling. Aimless. Eyes white with confusion and pain.

"All of them?" he said to Shaye. "You are going to lead all of them to their deaths?" Jonas knew "death" was the wrong word, but what else could he say. There were no words to properly describe what was before him now in the darkness.

"They will be free. No more pain. Nothing but peace."

Then Jonas looked again at the girl who had been his daughter.

Shaye pulled in closer to him, a spectre of a man. A walking ghost. "Do you plan to stand in my way this time, Burke?"

Jonas looked at the frail man, who did not seem so threatening now. He seemed only . . . vulnerable. And afraid.

"No," Jonas said. The word like a stone in his throat.

In the corner, Victor sat, back against the wall, the undead swarming around him, those who could talk peppering him with half-formed questions, those who could not, simply listening. For him, they would do anything. He was their leader, their fallen idol. Their prophet. He had become the Messiah of the Undead.

For him, they would willingly walk into fire.

Shaye nodded toward Victor and smiled. "I'm surprised—and quite frankly a little disappointed—that he did not kill you. You must have spun quite a web of excuses in order to get his hands from around your Adam's apple."

"There is no excuse for what I did," said Jonas. "And that is just exactly what I told him. Lucias Angel played me for a fool once again."

"You are really starting to make a habit of that."

"Desperate men make ill-advised decisions, Shaye. But I sincerely believed that Angel would never do anything to harm, Victor. He promised me. He told me Victor held the answer to saving Jillian. That by bringing him back from the Arctic, my girl could be saved. I could not have predicted how any of this would have turned out. But Angel's duplicity has only increased my resolve to see this thing through. To make certain Angel is stopped."

"You will most likely die long before any of this comes to pass. You are aware of that?"

"My life ended the day she drew her last breath," Jonas said, staring at the girl with the blonde hair and faraway eyes. The girl he had lost. "I do not fear Lucias Angel."

"That is good," Shaye said. "Because he will come after you like a hound of hell. And he will not come alone. Victor has told us he has already found himself a new Bone Welder. One who appears to find a great amount of satisfaction in his work. Whether you fear Angel or not, be assured that he will find some way to get to you. Some way."

"I have nothing left."

Shaye squinted. "You know the truth of what I am saying. He will find your weakness and he will burrow into it like a cancer. If you try to fight him, to stop him, to get in his way, Jonas, he will get to you. And he will make it hurt."

HOME SWEET HOME.

WALTON WALLACE COULD NOT WAIT to wash the filth of travel from his body. God, how he hated it. The pushing, heaving bodies that filled the airports and the bursting planes. The rude clerks, the delays, the black feeling of isolation and disconnection.

Back in his apartment he felt whole again. Grounded. He slumped into the chair in his front room, still wearing a suit and tie that strangled him, and stared out into the cold Chicago night. It was a starless night, the air outside as frigid as razor blades.

In the streets below, red taillights winked behind an endless string of cars.

He rubbed his eyes. Sighed. He thought about clicking the television to life but decided against it. He had to get up; he needed a shower. And if he turned on the tube, he knew he would sit here half the night, hypnotized.

He loosened his tie, something he should have done long ago, and leaned back in the chair. He closed his eyes.

It would have been only natural for him to drift quickly into slumber; he was, after all, exhausted. Drained.

But he couldn't sleep. Because a black scratching uncertainty had formed at the back of his mind. A small round marble of panic.

Something was different about the apartment. Something was *wrong*.

There was a pallid scent in the air. One that did not belong in his home. It smelled of desperation. The damp animal musk of terror and fear.

"Jonas," he said quietly, although in the stillness of the apartment his voice sounded enormous. He expected no answer. He knew the apartment was empty. He could feel it.

Walton searched room to room for any sign of his guests. But there were none. They had left the place spotless. Better than Walton had remembered it ever looking before. Typical for Jonas, he thought. He had been the best architect at his firm, perhaps not the most creative, but always the most thorough and contemplative. Jonas Burke turned in no work until it was perfect. And it was why Walton recommended Jonas to everyone he knew. Not because they were friends, but because he was the best.

In the bedroom, the bed linens and comforter had been pulled tight and even smoothed out flat by hand. Walton smiled.

The kitchen was much the same. All the dishes in the sink had been cleaned and put away. Countertops polished. Floor swept.

In the small living room, the pillows on the couch and chairs had been placed with precision.

Everything looked perfect.

So what was wrong, he wondered. Why did a diamond hard tingle of dread nudge at the base of his skull?

His cell phone buzzed, and Walton jumped, startled. Oh Christ, he thought immediately. Judith. He had forgotten to call her last night—the business dinner had gone on so long—and now he had neglected to call her tonight. He was going to hear about it.

He pulled the phone from his suit jacket pocket and immediately began talking. "Honey, listen . . . "But all he heard by way of reply was dead air. Static. Or maybe it was something else. Not static, perhaps. Maybe . . . breathing.

He glanced quickly at the caller ID, which said only: Unknown Number.

He quickly dialed Judith's number.

He prepared his apology as it rang on the other end. And rang. Eight times. Nine. Walton sighed and clicked the connection closed. She must have gone out. Was probably mad and needed some fresh air. Walton knew how Judith could get, how she could hold a grudge for days—weeks— on end. He had an uphill battle ahead.

Walton returned to the kitchen and swung open the refrigerator door. He was a little surprised at the disarray he saw there. He supposed even Jonas had his limits.

Walton reached behind a gallon of milk and came away with a Sam Adams lager, pearls of condensation snaking down the brown bottle. He twisted the top free and drank deeply. He could feel the wear and tear of the past few days slip away, his muscles easing, melting.

For a moment he stood, the only light in the apartment coming from the front hallway. He watched the shadows, grey and steely, as they shifted around him. Then shift again. His heart raced.

"Is someone there?" he asked. Immediately, he felt stupid. But . . .

He could not shake the dizzying feeling of vertigo. The nauseating sensation that he was in his own apartment, but that it was *not* really his. Someone else had tampered with it. Violated it.

The sudden realization that he had forgotten to deadbolt the door upon coming home sent rivulets of fear spiraling through him. He crossed slowly into the hallway, fought the electric tingle of horror as he clicked the lock into place. It was almost like he could feel a presence on the other side of the door. Waiting to come in. Like Walton had made it just in time before . . .

His phone buzzed again. Walton yelped. Not loudly. Like that of a frightened shelter dog. He could not control it. This was crazy, he told himself. He had to get in the shower. He needed to calm down. He could not stand in this apartment for the rest of the night leaping out of his skin at shadows. This time he hoped it was Judith. It would be nice to hear her voice. Nice to hear something familiar.

Unknown Number

He tapped the Talk button.

"Who is this?"

Again, nothing but static. That's what it was, wasn't it? Just static?

Then he saw it. In the hallway.

It was so subtle. Nearly imperceptible. But there it was. Right next to him. Like a cold whisper.

In the narrow hallway, Walton had decorated both walls with pictures that held special meaning to him. Lots of pictures. All framed in soft gold. Some black and white. Many other color. Pictures of his mother and father. Of his sister. And childhood friends. Photos of his senior class trip to Washington, DC, and others of his family's vacations to the Grand Canyon, Disneyworld, Paris. Scores of pictures. They were the only things in the apartment he kept neat, the only thing someone like Jonas Burke would not need to tamper with. He always kept them straight. And dusted.

But tonight, there was something just a bit out of kilter. A little different. There was an extra photograph. One that he had never seen before. One that he had not put on his wall.

It was just above a small curio table he kept by the door to hold his keys and the day's mail. It was mixed in unobtrusively amongst all the other pictures.

Walton had known something was wrong. Had felt it like an electric current. And here it was. He squinted. And then leaned into the photograph.

His heart thundered, blood surging into his ears, an ocean of blood filling his senses. My God, it was Judith. A photograph of Judith.

It was her but . . . something had been done to her. She had been . . . altered. At first he assumed it had been a trick photo. Maybe something that had been digitally doctored. Then he saw her face. The terror in her eyes, the pleading sadness that crouched there in her faraway stare. The shock that had turned her ashen and slack-jawed.

Walton pulled in closer. So hard to see. The phone came to life again. Started to vibrate in his hand. Buzzed and buzzed. Like it was never going to end.

He did not notice as the beer bottle slid from his hand and crashed to the hardwood floor below. He did not bristle at the sound of glass shattering. He could only look at the picture, turn his head, before screaming.

His hands trembled as he clamped them to his temples, the phone still buzzing like a hornet. He shook his head, back and forth. Violently. Trying to shake free the image of Judith. The image of Judith from the photo. It had looked so normal at first. So innocuous. But then Walton had studied it. Had looked closely into its hidden shadows. She sat on a stool, face contorted in pain and confusion. Eyes welling with tears. Her legs shot out straight in front of her, stiff. But that was not so unusual. Not at all.

What *was* unusual were her arms. Walton looked and looked. Then the screaming began. Her arms were cocked at the elbows, hands resting on knees. But the arms were too big, a little too sinewy. And there was hair.

A man's arms.

And there were scars.

Walton continued to scream. For how long he could not say. But when he stopped, the phone was still buzzing. Trilling like a wailing infant. He clicked the phone line open. Starbursts of adrenaline shooting beyond his eyes. The phone felt cold in his hand, lifeless. He said nothing as he brought it to his ear.

This time there was a voice. Not static. But a voice.

And it spoke to him.

DARK MYSTERIES.

JONAS HAD SPENT too much time amongst the dead. He needed air. Space. Away from the gray-eyed hulks beneath the zoo.

He needed to feel alive.

And the night-drenched city streets of Chicago could provide just the shot of adrenaline he needed. He walked south along Michigan Avenue, past storefronts that glittered in the tranquil darkness of night. The wind tore at him with icy claws, and yet it was not bitter, not painful. In fact, Jonas stopped for a while, the stream of pedestrian traffic surging around him, and turned his face up into the sky, allowing the air to pour over him, a frigid caress.

So many memories here, Jonas thought. Happy memories. But the sad truth of life, Jonas had learned, was that the happier the memory, the greater than pain when recalling it. He and Katherine had fallen in love in this city. Had first held hands walking along the lakefront at North

Street Beach, the summer sun warming them. Had dined in all the fancy restaurants along Michigan Avenue and Oak Street and the funky, trendy spots, as well, in the Lincoln Park area.

They had known such joy then. The kind of happiness only the young experience but do not know enough to appreciate.

Jonas knew suddenly where he needed to go, where he could find some solace. He cut across Michigan Avenue and headed two blocks west, the crisp lights of the Magnificent Mile behind him.

Up ahead, a corner bar buzzed smoothly with the gentle murmuring of friends drinking and laughing. Next door, the soft lights of an all-night coffee house washed out onto the sidewalk.

And then, Jonas saw his destination, happy to find it still in business. He pushed the door to the Dark Mysteries Bookstore inward and stepped into the hushed silence. Long ago, when Jonas had known happiness, when Jonas had a family and friends and a future, this is what he enjoyed most. Browsing through the bookstores of Chicago. The new stores, with racks and racks of titles he dreamed of diving into, but especially the used bookstores. Dusty and dark, holding onto their buried treasures like long-dead secrets.

Jonas walked slowly through the cramped aisles, titles stacked atop one another, leaning, falling, holding onto one another. An explosion of books, running riot.

At last his hand came to rest upon an old Ballantine paperback of *The Illustrated Man*, the cover blaring as red as the surface of Mars. His heart raced. It had been years—long, long years—since first reading it. Jonas yanked it quickly from the shelf as if a delay might cause it to disappear before his very eyes, as if it would vanish like mist before he had a chance to hold it in his hands.

Jonas climbed the winding iron stairs to the second floor and plopped down into an oversized chair beside a display of children's books. He cracked open the book and began to read. Bradbury was comforting to him. And familiar. Like settling down with an old friend. He read "The Veldt" and smiled again at its delicious comeuppance. Then he savored "Kaleidoscope," all the while fighting to remember the feelings he experienced the first time he read it, so many years ago, filled with awe and wonder at its imagination and heart, back before his wife had died, back before his daughter had been taken from him.

Back before everything.

It wasn't until he was halfway through "The Long Rain" that the air inside the bookstore changed. Seemed to grow colder. Then a shadow fell over the book in Jonas's lap.

"Bradbury?" a voice said. "I took you for much more mainstream, Burke. Clancy perhaps. Or Grisham."

Jonas needn't look up to identify the speaker. He knew the voice. Lucias Angel dropped into a chair opposite Jonas. He wore a long, flowing black coat that swirled around him like a cape. His black hair, darker than a thousand midnights, was pulled into a ponytail.

Jonas leaned forward. "What's to stop me from screaming for the cops right now?"

Angel laughed. "And tell them what? That I'm bringing the dead back to life and you would like me to cease and desist right this moment? Really, Burke, idle threats are not becoming of you."

"Why have you followed me? What do you want? You betrayed me once. Isn't that enough?"

"I could not tell you everything. That is not betrayal; that is simply good business. Even you should understand that. I couldn't tell you my plans for Victor, as he calls himself. I knew things had the potential to get . . . ugly."

"And that does not bother you? Hacking your own brother to pieces?"

"Sometimes we must do things we find distasteful so that we may reach a higher truth."

Jonas huffed. "But there is no higher truth. Don't you see? That's what your experiments have shown. Death is the end. As it has been since the beginning of time. As it was meant to be."

"Of course, and man was meant to die of Scarlet Fever and the Bubonic plaque and be crippled by polio. We should never tamper with the impenetrable forces of Mother Nature, isn't that right? We should just let things be."

Jonas gently closed the book on his lap, and set it down on a coffee table next to him already half full with discarded magazines and books other casual readers had left behind.

"What do you want?"

Lucias folded his long, bird-like fingers beneath his chin. "I want Victor."

"And you think I will bring him to you? After what you have already done."

Lucias smiled. Like a crocodile. All teeth and caged fury. "Again, sometimes we have to do things we are uncomfortable with, if only that we may achieve greatness in the process." Still smiling. "Or avoid pain."

Jonas bristled at the implied threat. "Are you through? I would like to get back to my book."

"You show no fear. I like that. Even if it is a bluff."

"I have nothing to fear from you. I am beyond pain."

Lucias laughed again. "My God, you are like something out of an old Western. Flinging platitudes around with a straight face. Jonas, my dear boy, no one is beyond pain. That is another of life's nasty little secrets."

Lucias reached inside his coat, fumbled through the black folds of cashmere and returned with a deep onyx cell phone, nearly as slim as a piece of paper. He turned the screen toward Jonas.

Jonas went cold. Immediately. He cursed himself for being so callous with Lucias, so disdainful. He should have known better than to play games with a man like Lucias Angel.

Angel held the phone toward Jonas, steadily, wedged between two razor-thin fingers. Held it there. Hand still as stone. Waiting for Jonas to respond. To look up at the screen.

Jonas fought the fear that clamored up his throat. Then, snake-quick, he glanced up at the phone, quickly, quickly, before he lost his nerve.

Lucias Angel, of course, had been correct. Jonas Burke was not exempt from pain. Far from it. And if anyone could locate a source of someone's suffering, and then exploit it, it was Lucias Angel.

The picture on the phone was fuzzy, badly lit, the colors all bleeding to red. But the subject was unmistakable. Walton Wallace. His oldest friend on earth. Silver strands of duct tape pinned him to a metal examining table. Around the wrists and ankles and around his neck. His eyes were wide, mostly white, pupils shrunk to pinpricks. And next to the table was a tray of gleaming instruments. Sharp, metal, waiting for flesh.

"I have additional photos of Mr. Wallace's girlfriend, as well, should you care to see them. My associates were, shall we say, *creative* in their treatment of her."

"I give you Victor and you release Walton, is that the deal? Unharmed?"

"Bring him to me. It will be best for everyone. You'll see. You are helping to further a great cause." Lucias rose, slipping the phone back inside his coat. So elegant, Jonas could not help thinking as he looked at the man. Dressed in the most expensive clothes the city's tailors and designers had to offer, perfectly groomed, hair immaculate, shoes polished, fingernails even buffed and trimmed.

"Know one thing, Jonas. If you do not come to me with what I want, I will come to you. There will be nowhere you can hide from me."

"Then why not just get Victor yourself?"

A dark smile wavered on Angel's face. "I don't always enjoy doing things the hard way. Not always. You have one chance. Then pain will follow."

Lucias nodded toward the book in Jonas's lap. "Try *Dark Carnival* some time. Some really creepy stuff. Might provide you with a shiver or two."

Lucias turned to leave.

"Does it bother you?" Jonas asked. "What you are doing to him? Strange as it is, you are brothers. You share the same father. In a world that hates and fears the two of you, you're all one another has. Are you not ashamed of what you have done to him?"

Jonas half-expected Lucias to flash that sour, plastic grin he had grown quickly to loathe. But he did not smile. Instead he glared, eyes as black as a witch's cauldron.

"Jonas, poor fool, I'm afraid you are one of those who insists on going through life with blinders on. And God knows, there are already enough people like that in the world. Try to be different. Try to think, for a change. My brother? He is much more than that. Much more. Victor Frankenstein was in no state of mind to create another being after he unleashed The Monster upon the world. That was left to someone else."

Jonas began to stammer, to object to what Lucias was about to say, but the words turned to dust in his mouth.

For in that moment, he knew the terrible truth that had been right in front of him this whole time. As obvious as death itself.

"Your friend Victor created me, Burke. Or should I say, brought me back from the dead. Maybe you should ask him about it. Probably make a great story."

Then the wicked smile was back. Lucias's teeth flashing like dull razors as he walked away from Jonas, vanishing into the black shadows.

"For you see, he is not my brother," Lucias said. "Victor is my *father*."

SLUMBERING.

IT WAS INCHING TOWARD TEN O'CLOCK when Jonas pushed out through the double doors of the bookstore. He turned back toward Michigan Avenue, and with the wind at his face, headed north. The city darkened palpably as he crossed over Oak Street and left the Magnificent Mile. The glow of the boutiques, upscale jewelry stores, pastry shops, cafes and the shining Water Tower shopping mall vanished in the distance. Subtly. Misty funhouse images in a rearview mirror.

Streetlights became less frequent and shadows welled up like oil spills in every alleyway, in the stoop of every brownstone, in the milky entryway to every apartment building. It amazed Jonas just how dark a city as big as Chicago could get.

He made his way along the outskirts of Lincoln Park. In the middle of the day, the park was perhaps the safest haven in the entire city. In the summer it was filled to overflowing with joggers, bikers, rollerbladers, sunbathers, walkers, readers, picnickers, dog walkers. But that was during the day.

At night, it was different. At night, everything in the city was different. Trees that provided shade in the day, provided hiding and camouflage at night. The happiness and smiles that filled this park in the sun's light were but wavering memories in the darkness. No more substantial than fog.

And there were people out in this park at night, too. Only they could not be seen. Some slept on park benches, tucked beneath today's discarded newspapers. Others lay behind rows of bushes. Others beneath the canopy of trees.

Others did not sleep at all. They waited. In the darkness.

Jonas walked briskly. He could feel the presence of the people in the park. He knew they were watching him, weighing him in their minds. All asking themselves the same question, Was he worth their effort?

Fortunately, Jonas was dressed no better than the homeless rabble who filled the night streets. He did not feel any great need to worry. But he thought of those young urban professionals, still wearing their Italian cut suits, ties loosened, as they stumbled from the bars along Division Street. Many of them would stumble up here, emboldened by the booze, feeling indestructible. When the people in the park watched them, smiling, peering out of the darkness, they would flash into movement.

Bloody and quick.

At the north end of the park, squatting in the dappled shadows, was the Lincoln Park Zoo. Jonas walked past. He knew Victor would not be there. He was as uncomfortable in the presence of Lucias's experiments as was Jonas.

He continued north, the wind now becoming particularly ravenous, turning the tips of his ears and nose raw. To his right, he could see the distant twinkle of the inky black waters of Lake Michigan, colder than a thousand-year-old tomb. He pulled his coat tight around his neck. He was getting close; that was comfort to him at least.

He turned toward the lake. A small residential area—squat, little, two-story buildings so tight they looked to have gone through a compactor—edged Lake Shore Drive. On the opposite side, mired in darkness, was a cemetery. A carved metal sign, Gothic and haunting, arched over the entryway. It read: Hollow Hills. Jonas walked underneath. The cemetery was thick with trees, thicker still with gravestones. Like rotten teeth the markers jutted up from the earth. Many of the stones were cracked and gnarled with age. At the far end of the cemetery, beneath the curled, ragged fingers of a towering elm tree, was a mausoleum, darkened from the centuries, ivy clinging to it like a disease. Leaning against the stone was Victor. He did not look up as Jonas approached. Not even when Jonas sat down hard on the ground beside him.

"You know, they say you can judge a man by the company he keeps," Jonas said.

"I prefer the companionship of the dead," Victor said, and then, almost as an afterthought, "the truly dead, that is."

"You'll get no argument from me. It is pretty cold out here, though. Nice warm bed doesn't sound half bad."

"I presumed after a century in the Arctic that Chicago would be more bearable. I was wrong."

Jonas tried in vain to find a comfortable position. The ground was bone hard beneath him, frozen tufts of grass cutting into him. The wall of the mausoleum at his back was colder than the Grim Reaper's touch, sapping the warmth from his body, what little remained.

In the distance, he could hear a dog barking, then another. And another. Then howling. Looking around the desolate cemetery, the lights of the city a dim memory, he had to remind himself that he was in Chicago and not thrown back in time to some quiet remote English Village. The howling continued, and then a shadow skittered across the frozen ground. The wind snapped the branches of the barren trees. Crack, crack, snap. Death-black shadows, cast from the obscenely twisted tree branches, darted amongst the tombstones like cobalt demons, shapeshifting, moving, crawling, changing shape again.

"He came to me tonight," Jonas said.

"As we knew he would."

"He wants me to deliver you to him."

"As we knew he would."

"He told me something. A secret."

The Monster sighed. "I'm sure he did not tell you everything."

"Why don't you?"

"It's not a story the world has ever shown any interest in. Shelley's tale is more compelling. A rampaging brute—a byproduct of death itself—roaming the countryside, killing without remorse, without pause. What could be more interesting than that?"

Jonas stared into Victor's solemn eyes. "The truth, Victor. Tell me the truth. What really happened all those years ago?"

"Why should I tell you?"

"Because I am willing to listen."

Victor tilted his head to the rabid wind, closed his eyes. Quietly, Jonas watched him. In the charcoal darkness, Jonas could not see the scars, could not see the mismatched hands, could see only the dignity. And the sorrow.

And the humanity.

Then Frankenstein's Monster spoke.

THE MONSTER'S TALE.

I WAS BORN TO THE SOUND OF THUNDER, and baptized in the bone-searing pain of electricity. My eyes opened for the first time to a world consumed by darkness, to heavens roiling with oily clouds, blacker than a raven's wing, deeper than the devil's own soul.

"It's alive," he screamed. My master. My creator. My father. And yet I did not feel alive.

I felt only cold.

And alone.

The product of a charnel house, pieced together with tatters of flesh. Sewn together, a patchwork, from bodies rank with the stench of death, pulled unwilling from the ground, white and bloated with the grave.

I was alive, true, but equally was I dead.

I was abhorrent; this I knew immediately. For only a monster would be shunned by his own father. Only a beast, a ghastly affront to God, could be neglected the love of a parent.

His name: Victor Frankenstein. His story is known well, but little is truly understood. His motivations can be speculated—as they have—but who can truly say what dark thoughts ran through his brain? And how it all began?

From his early days, he was influenced by the works of Cornelius Agrippa, and then later by Paracelsus and Albertus Magnus. Electricity and galvanism pre-occupied him day and night. And later, at the University of Ingolstadt, his black ideas turned solid. Made flesh.

I can recall awakening into that dusty, damp, cubbyhole of a room, laid out flat on a slab of wood, surrounded by the trappings of his mad science; beakers and test tubes, microscopes and specimen jars, some filled with small animals—toads, mice, cockroaches—others with human parts—hands, eyeballs, genitalia.

My father's reaction as his creation opened its eyes for the first time upon the world? Ah, yes. A strangled horror. Gasping for air, pupils wide, mortified. If that was to be the reaction of my father, what hope did I have in the world? Who would ever love such a creature?

And so he abandoned me. Bolted from the room like one of hell's furies. Still too horrified to so much as even scream. I lay for a while, confused, afraid. Alone. Staring up at the ceiling. Finally, I pulled myself to my feet, taking my first tentative steps, a newborn coughed from the grave. It was dark, nighttime. The only light from a small lantern in the corner, wheezing yellow illumination in a weak circle around it. There was also a small window, and beyond the window more darkness.

I was frozen with fear. Now what was I to do? I knew nothing, understood nothing. I did not know where I was. I did not even know *who* I was.

Humans cry when they are afraid. Or they scream out. I simply walked about the room, shuffling, eyes closed. Trying to think. Think.

Along the back wall was a small, slanted table. Scraps of paper littered its surface, black ink splattered like gunshots. And also, a mirror.

I went to it. Uncertain. I had caught glimpses of myself in it as I walked furtively about the room, but now I moved very deliberately to it. Stopped. And looked deep into the well of my own reflection.

I looked at my face, turned the mirror slowly, to make certain that it was really *me*, and not some stranger staring back, toying with me.

I searched every line of my face, every scar, every wrinkle and pockmark and blemish, and yet I could not understand what it was about me that was so horrendous. So grotesque. I decided that my father must have been frightened of something else. Or perhaps he was simply exhausted with the efforts of bringing me to life.

I had misunderstood him; that's what my feeble mind told me. He did not hate me. Not at all. He was my father.

And so I went to him. How I found him, I am still unsure. Those first memories remain scattered and obtuse, like looking back at the past through a fogged window.

But find him I did, lying in his bed, drenched in his own cold sweat, face twisted in anguish. Then he saw me, standing over him. I reached out to touch him, to soothe him. His pain caused me pain and I wanted only to comfort him. I wanted him to realize the deepness of my humanity, that I was not a thing to be feared and scorned.

I wanted him to see that I was a man.

But it was not to be. Not then, not ever. He rebuked me again. Screaming. Eyes wild with terror. He dashed from the room. And I would not see him again—my father—for two years.

Like the fallen angel thrown from the grace of Heaven I wandered blind and unknowing through a world that did not want me.

In the dark forest near Ingolstadt I found refuge. I stumbled through the cathedral of trees, searching, but for what I could not say. One day, I came upon a small hut belonging to an old man, hunting and fishing for his sustenance. I approached, stood at the door and waited for him to take notice. He did. And his screams were even louder than those of my creator. Heart-wrenching and filled with black dread, his yells sent birds bursting to flight from the surrounding trees. Then he fainted away.

For months I hid in the blue-black shadows of the forest, too ashamed to show my face.

I did nothing. Did not sleep. Did not eat. Just lay on the soft pine needles that blanketed the ground, listening to the quiet tittering of the birds, watching the sky, some days a blue deeper than an angel's soul, others dark as death itself.

And I roamed. With no destination in mind. I just needed to move. To pretend, even if only for my own self-deluded satisfaction, that I was alive.

Then, on a cloudy morning in late fall, a mist of cold rain trickling from a sorrowful sky, I came upon a small village. I watched the quiet little people as they shuffled through the mud, baskets dangling from the crooks in their arms, smiling at one another as they passed.

And as I watched them, strange thoughts came to me. Perhaps these people will be different, I thought. Perhaps they will not recoil from me, screaming. Another dark thought: What if my master's reaction had been more the effect of his own twisted mind rather than as a reaction to me? Perhaps he was insane, his mind rattled and darkened by his experiments. And the old man? A hobbled hermit, locked away in the woods, solitary. Perhaps his mind had slipped from its moorings, as well.

A man can delude himself in unimaginable ways when he is pressed. I wanted nothing more than human companionship, and I convinced myself that it was possible. I could not be as miserable a creature as my creator would have me believe.

And so I walked from the shadows. Hesitantly. Eyes darting from person to person as I entered the village. For a few blissful moments, I remained unnoticed. I walked amongst them, head down, as they bustled through their daily chores. But that, I'm afraid, could not last.

I saw a pair of feet before me, small, bound in tattered leather. I raised my head. It was a little girl, no more than seven or eight. She stood transfixed for a moment, mouth agape, a solemn twitching in her fingers. Then she turned and fled, a piercing wail escaping her lips. She tripped and thumped to the ground, mud forming waves around her. She never stopped screaming. The other villagers dashed to her side. Others pounded from within their huts, drying hands on dirty rags, adjusting clothing, patting matted hair flat. They looked at her, eager to help, frightened, confused as to what had caused her such distress. Then her eyes led them to me. They looked up. Stood. Said nothing. But they did not have to. I could see it in their worn faces. The abject terror. The repulsion.

I felt a fool for having convinced myself that their reaction would have been any different. For having convinced myself that I could walk among men.

I turned to descend again into the darkness of the forest. A sharp pain. I fell to my knees. Head throbbing. Another jolt of pain, even greater than the first, and I then noticed a rock tumble to rest at my feet. Then another sailed over my head and crashed to the ground. Another. Another.

I got to my feet and ran, once looking back over my shoulder to see an army of villagers, faces twisted into scowls, as they pelted me with rocks, and sticks, and mounds of their own human waste.

And so I slunk away, like some vermin, a cockroach. "All men hate the wretched," Shelley has me say at one point in her story, "how, then, must I be hated, who am miserable beyond all living things." Whether or not I truly spoke these words is unimportant. They reflect clearly the way in which I felt.

Hated. Feared.

Wretched.

Not far from the village, there was another small cottage, and next to it, a small, abandoned lean-to with an earthen floor. It was dilapidated from lack of use and care, but I made it my home. Winter would be rumbling in soon, filling the sky with its gray, snow-pregnant clouds. This lean-to, miserable as it was, would at least keep me dry.

In the morning, the sounds of humans again reached my ears. Muffled conversation, coughing, laughing. There was a family inside the cottage. A father, and his two children whose names, I would come to learn, were Felix and Agatha. Through a narrow gap in the wood of the cottage, I could watch them. And that is what I did. For months. And months. They played music together and sang. And late at night, under the glow of a quiet lantern Felix would read poetry to his father and sister. Such beautiful words, I thought. And so I learned language. And in time, after stealing away with their books under cover of night, I learned to read.

Late at night, while the family—DeLacey was their surname—would sleep, I foraged through the forest for food I could leave on their doorstep. They were so terribly poor, but they had love, companionship.

One night, cold, I remember it being so bitterly cold, I stumbled upon a portmanteau containing several books.

Beautiful, leather-bound, smelling of soft wood and incense. I read them all. Then again. And again. Goethe's *Sorrows of Young Werther*. Plutarch's *Lives*. And finally, and most importantly, Milton's *Paradise Lost*. In Milton's words I tried to discover myself. As he described Man's creation, and fall, and then eventual reunion with his creator, I wondered if he could have been speaking of me. Was that to be my fate? Would an omnipotent and ultimately benevolent God, or creator, welcome me into his arms again someday?

Or was I simply like God's other creation, which he casts aside, rejects, never to lay claim to again. Satan.

Which was I, I thought. Which was I?

Finally, unable to withstand the loneliness a moment longer, the dreadful, cursed solitude, I waited for Felix and Agatha to leave and then cautiously I approached the cottage. I knocked on the door. A voice from inside said, "Who is it? Felix, is that you?" Then shuffling feet as the old man came toward the door.

But I did not fear. For the old man, sweet and gentle as any soul could be, was also blind.

The door moaned inward. The old man stood, a smile hung on his face like a crooked painting. "Who's there? May I help you?"

"I . . . I . . ." I tried to speak but having never used my voice before, other than to scream in pain and sorrow, the words cramped in my throat, sinking their claws into me.

"Are you okay? Do you need help?" The old man asked.

"The . . . food. The . . ."

221

"Do you need food? Is that what you would like? You should come in, my friend. You sound like you have had a difficult journey." And then he reached out for me. I recoiled, afraid. He would hate me if he knew, if he could see the monster that I was. But instead he wrapped his old fingers, weak with age, around my coat sleeve and beckoned me in again. It was the first time I had felt a kind human touch before. The first time someone had expressed concern for me, kindness, instead of hatred and fear.

It was also the last.

He led me inside. He started toward the fire, and the cauldron that hung there, boiling with soup. I stopped him. "No," I said. "I do not . . . do not desire food. I was trying to say that it was I . . . who had left the offerings at your door. The roots, and berries and mushrooms."

"Ah," the man explained. "Is that who you are? We owe a great debt. Indeed, we do. Your kindness has saved us from hunger on many evenings. But why have you done this? Surely you have your own family to tend to."

"No," I replied. "I do not. I see the love that you have for one another. I hope I have helped you." I was becoming more comfortable with my voice now.

"What is your name?" the old man asked.

A simple question, and yet how could I answer? My creator had been so repulsed by me that he had not even seen fit to give me a name. Every man deserves a name. Even a monster passing himself off as one. "Victor," I said. "After my father."

"Well, Victor, I am so pleased to have you here. Please, please sit. You will at least have a cigar with me, yes." The old man did not wait for a reply. He retrieved two cigars from the table beside the fire and nimbly lit them, moving as confidently as any man blessed with sight. I watched him as he puffed voraciously, filling the room with the sweet white smoke, a cloud forming around his face, obscuring him, a ghost. I inhaled slowly, held the smoke for a moment, and let it out in an explosion of coughing.

The old man laughed. "Sorry, my friend. They are perhaps not the finest cigars in all the world. I'm afraid the poor must make do with what the good Lord provides them."

"No, not at all. They are very good."

"Tell me, Victor. What is it you are doing out in these woods? They are no place for a young man like yourself."

"They are my home."

"You have a cottage then? Nearby? I am surprised that neither of my children have ever seen it."

"It is easy to miss," I said.

The fire was warm, filling the room with a soft, easy glow. Like an orange sunset. The cigar felt good, as well, sweet and pungent, taking the raw edge of cold from my bones.

And for those brief few moments, I knew happiness. I knew peace. I was a man.

Then the old man's children returned.

Neither of us heard them approach. Felix was first through the door, followed by his sister. Such a handsome pair. Beautiful, strong children.

"What are you doing? Who are you?" Felix screamed. His father, alarmed, tried to soothe his son, having, of course, no idea what had driven him to such behavior.

"Felix, please," said the old man. "Do not be rude. This is guest. A friend of mine. His name is . . ."

Felix waited for no more explanation from his father. Instead, he lunged. He brought the full force of his body against my chest, knocking me to the floor. He proceeded then to kick me, hard, viciously, his boot crashing into my chin, thudding against my ribs. There was pain, but nothing I could not endure. It was his words that carried the greatest sting.

"Monster. Horrible abomination. Vile creature. Animal. Beast. Monster."

Then again. "Monster. Monster."

How could he say such things to me? How could his anger and hatred be so great when he had never before laid eyes upon me? Does not a man deserve to be judged by something other than his outward appearance?

I could feel an anger well inside me then, burn like fire, choking me. I jumped to my feet, blind with fury. When next I have memory, I was standing in the middle of the small cottage, my hands choking the life out of Felix, the poor young man flailing helplessly, gasping for breath, his sister screaming from the corner of the room, the old man lost, confused, tears in his eyes. I could have killed him — I wanted to, so much did I now revile mankind as much as it reviled me—but I did not.

I ran, the echoes of Agatha's searing yells chasing after me.

For days, I wandered through those dark woods, lost and confused. A profound sadness threatened to drive me to the edge of despair.

It was then I stumbled upon a book. I had discovered it, well-worn and tattered, in my coat pocket months before. But this had occurred long before I had any understanding of the written language, and so I had set it aside.

Now, in the quiet hours beyond midnight, a full moon blooming high above the canopy of trees, I pulled it from the spot in which it had been hidden and turned the sodden leather over in my hands.

It was, I then realized, more than just a book. It was a journal.

I shuddered when I read the legend written across its surface in a shaking, maddening hand.

The Journal of Doctor Victor Frankenstein, it read. And then, underneath: *The Reconstitution and Resurrection of Life*.

I ran my finger across the coarseness of its leather cover, a tremble rattling my fingers.

Then I pulled open the musty tome and began to read. By the time I had read but a few pages a dread as black as a thousand midnights filled my soul. And, for a moment, I thought I might go mad.

Or that, perhaps, I already had.

And what did I find in those dark pages that so tormented me?

The truth. That is what I found.

The horrid truth.

For you see, all that I have told you to this point about my origin — being sewn together with discarded remnants of the dead, jolted to "life" with a current of electricity — all of this I learned from the terrible journal that quivered in my hand.

I can relate these events to you now because of what I uncovered then, sitting alone in the quiet woods, all those years ago, reading the diary of my father.

My creator.

Until then I knew nothing of how I was created, of the horror of my "birth." I knew, of course, that I was a horror for others to behold. How could I not? The reactions of those who saw me assured me of that. But I did not know why?

Why did the villagers curl their lips at my approach? Why did they snatch up their children in their arms and scramble for shelter? Why?

Now I had the answer.

I now knew my origin. I was spit from the graves of the freshly dead, an abomination to nature.

I was a monster.

I dropped the journal onto the soft bed of pine needles at my feet, and tried to cry. To shed tears for the shame and horror I felt. But I could not. For a monster cannot cry.

My back to the trunk of a large tree, I sat on the cold ground. My mind filled with images too horrid to share. Too painful to endure.

If I was not already insane, then surely I soon would be.

I sat alone in the dark woods, unwanted by all who had ever seen me. And I realized then that I was to be this way forever. For eternity. Because since I was not truly alive, I could never really die. An eternity of loneliness.

Unless I did something about it.

And so, after some time had passed, I turned my attention back to the journal. I could not sit and wallow in the terror of what I had learned. No, I must find something else to occupy my drowning mind. Now that the true nature of my existence had been revealed to me, what else could I learn?

What else could my father teach me?

I steeled my nerves and under the ghostly light of a full moon, I cracked open the journal and read. Two hours later I had finished. Then I reread it, not every line, but certain passages that piqued my interest.

I remain uncertain as to exactly what I expected to discover in those disjointed, rambling pages. One thing was certain: Victor Frankenstein was not a madman. He was considered so, of course, by colleagues and professors who had learned of his work. His intentions, I believe, were honorable, however. He wished only to control that which, by its very nature, defies control—death itself.

His idealism was quickly shattered, though, when he saw what he had created, laid out on the table, drawing breath for the first time into its grave-robbed lungs.

Something else: I knew almost instantly the error that Frankenstein had made in his experiments. He should never have tried to "build" his own creation. That was pure folly. Digging through darkened churchyards, cutting loose dangling corpses from the hangman's noose, stitching and sewing together flesh that had already begun its sickening descent into rot. It was bad judgment. And perhaps, even worse, bad science.

No, the only way in which to truly gain dominion over the forces of life and death was to resurrect a corpse. Truly bring someone back from the dead, as whole as the day they drew their last breath.

And so that is what I set out to do.

I never asked for a bride, that was another literary conceit, though I admit there is some somber elegance in that idea. My intentions, as was often the case, were much simpler. I wished only to please my father. I thought that if I could glean the necessary elements of his own research but apply it in a different direction—to the resurrection of life as opposed to the creation of a sentient being—that my father would accept me into his good graces. He would view me as a success.

I would prove myself worthy of his love.

So I set to work. The university had one of Europe's most distinguished scientific labs, for use by student and faculty alike. Under the cover of darkness I began nightly visits to the lab, entering through a side door whose rusted padlock I was able to displace with a simple turn of the hand.

The laboratory contained everything I needed. With one exception: A body. The medical school had an attaching morgue, which held several cadavers, but the students had already begun their grisly studies on them. Ribs cracked open, flesh peeled back, scalps removed, tendons in the arms and legs severed. Nothing I could use.

I would have to find one on my own.

Shelley's story goes something like this: The Monster (myself) kills Baron Frankenstein's young brother William, and then plants evidence of the crime upon a family friend named Justine Moritz who is hanged for the crime. The Monster meets the Baron on a lonely mountainside and demands that he makes him a mate; if he does so, he will be left alone. The Baron travels to Scotland where he begins his dark experiments again. But he cannot continue, so disgusted is he in his prior creation and afraid that the two will mate and create a race of monsters to consume the world. He destroys the female companion, enraging the Monster who vows he will see the Doctor again on his wedding night. In the morning, Frankenstein's best friend, the dashing, charming Henry Clerval, is found strangled. The Beast has struck again. Then, of course, on Victor's wedding night, as promised, shrieks fill the great halls of Frankenstein castle as the fair Elizabeth, Dr. Frankenstein's bride-to-be, is throttled to death by the lumbering beast.

And ever since, I have had to bear the mark of murderer. I suppose it is a decent enough story, full of deceit and intrigue and horror but . . . that is just it; it is nothing more than a story. The truth . . . well, the truth is something different altogether. The young William was indeed murdered, as were Henry Clerval and Elizabeth, but the circumstances were even more bizarre than the legend. Perhaps that is why Shelley did not repeat it; she was afraid her tale would veer forever from the purely morbid into the realm of the totally unbelievable. A yarn so fanciful, not even the most open-minded reader would fall under its spell.

So here is the truth. For the first time. And for the last.

Henry Clerval and Victor Frankenstein were like brothers. As close to blood as two men could aspire. And although Clerval disagreed with the path of medicine his friend pursued so vigorously in his studies, he remained a loyal friend. That is how Victor Frankenstein perceived it, at least. The two had spent their entire lives together, playing as youth, chasing the ladies about in their adolescence, going off to university at the same time. Different universities, much to Victor Frankenstein's disappointment.

Later, after Victor had returned home, he indeed planned a trip to Scotland with Henry, but not to create a mate for me. The reason for the trip is unclear. Perhaps it was merely recreation, but there are reasons to believe that Frankenstein, while horrified by the results of his initial experiments, was again trying his hand at playing God. For he leased a small cottage in which he had placed a great deal of the scientific apparatus he had used at the university. Nonetheless, whatever Dr. Frankenstein had planned to accomplish in his new laboratory, everything changed within only a day or two of his arrival.

For soon, on a foggy morning, the lifeless body of his best friend Henry Clerval was discovered on the beach, strangled to death.

Doctor Frankenstein was questioned by police for some time, and as Shelley described in her book he caterwauled and objected and finally broke down and told authorities of the monster he had created. And that it was the beast, coughed from the grave, who had done this terrible dark deed. They thought him mad, of course. Yet, I have no doubt that at that time, his mind reeling into a darkness from which he would never return, he believed the story he told. He believed it was I who had murdered his dear friend.

The death of the dashing young Henry was indeed tragic, yet in his demise I saw my salvation. The body I so desperately needed for my own experiment had been handed me, seemingly from a benign deity, one whom I thought had turned His back on me forever.

The body was transported from Scotland to Geneva for burial. The night before the funeral, Clerval's corpse rested in the Holmgain Mortuary. In the morning, much to the consternation and surprise of his family and loved ones, the body of the beloved Henry Clerval was gone. Vanished into the misty evening. As if it had never existed.

Through oily alleyways, dense with shadows, I slunk back to the university, my trophy slung over my shoulder. I had prepared well, everything in place. And so, as the hands of the clock inched, crept, toward the witching hour of midnight, a violent storm thundered in from the north, and the night sky came alive with the fiery sentinels of electricity.

Lightning. Crisp and sharp.

And then, like Frankenstein himself must have felt in those first euphoric moments in which I first opened my eyes, I knew what it was like to be God.

Clerval came awake. Full. Complete. Not stitched together like some grotesque puppet. But whole. A man.

Alas, though, his brain—his poor feeble brain—was not much more capable of thought than was mine at the time of my rebirth. But I knew that would change. He could be taught. And I would gladly assume that role. Of teacher. Of mentor.

Of father.

We made our way to the woods, immediately. I wish that I could have provided more for him, but . . . that was not to be. Not now. The world was not ready for us. Or, should I say, it was not ready for me?

Henry, well . . . I suppose I realized immediately that we would never truly be soul mates. He would never truly, *truly*, understand my plight, my suffering. For Henry Clerval, clutched from the grasp of death itself and returned to earth, was beautiful. His flesh was whiter, that is true, and blemished around the neck, bruised from the violence of his death, but he was the furthest thing in the world from a monster. Once language returned to him, he would melt back into society without a care. Adored by women, as he had been in life, envied by men who lacked his handsome features.

I sound jealous. I know. And I suppose I am. From the beginning, I am sure that is true. In examining the errors my own creator had made in bringing me to life, such as it is, I was able to rectify and correct them all in my creation. And so the ghastly stitches were absent, as were the other grotesqueries; the mismatched hands, the discolored, mottled skin.

He was perfect. And, I suppose, in many ways I hated him for that.

But that was all the more reason for Doctor Frankenstein, the man who had opened my eyes to the world only to shun me, to accept me back into his graces. He would see the beauty of what I had done.

But I needed to work quickly. I must teach Henry at least the rudiments of the spoken language. And I had but three nights. For that is when Victor Frankenstein would take his dear Elizabeth as his wife.

And what better gift than to see his best friend again?

The storm intensified over the next two days, rain slashing from the black sky, thunder booming like cannon shot. In the miserable little lean-to that comprised my home, I tried to teach Henry the fundamentals of speaking. I read to him, slowly. Over and over. The same passages from my already well-worn volumes. Then I spoke to him, even more slowly, one word at a time, and he would grudgingly repeat them back.

It was a grueling process, but as he began to grasp several words (including the name "Victor") I felt a warm sensation of satisfaction. Doctor Frankenstein would have no choice other than to be impressed with my work.

The day before the wedding, however, the world nearly blackened beyond any recourse for me. Henry disappeared. Simply vanished into the frosted woods after nightfall. Where he could have gone, I had no idea.

What would happen if I could not find him? What would become of me? And of my father? I had come too far to fail so terribly. And so I ran through the forest, calling his name, black branches slashing at me, vines entangling my feet.

Hours passed. And nothing.

Winded, I sat upon a rock, slippery with moss, and lowered my head into my hands. With the tips of my fingers I could feel the pulpy ridges of scars that ran along my face and neck. Knotted flesh, lacerated. I pulled my hands away.

"V . . . Victor."

I looked up to see Henry, stock still, hands out. I asked him where he had gone, but he did not possess the resources to tell me. No matter; I had found him, or should I say, he had found me. Either way, we were together again. And now he was safe.

At last the night of the wedding arrived. The storm had settled over the land like some bleak malignancy, refusing to let anyone out of its grasp, pounding the earth with its fury. Through the stinging rain, Henry and I made our way to Castle Frankenstein.

A flood of humanity wound its way up to the portcullis, the landed gentry in their fine gold-accented carriages, safe and dry, the commoners slogging through the mud. We departed the main road, so as not to be seen, and made our way slowly up toward the dark castle by way of the surrounding woods. As we did so, we became immediately aware of a light in the distance. As we drew nearer, the source of the light sharpened and became more clear. It was a giant, twenty-foot-high window, trimmed with stained glass, through which could be seen a splendid bedroom suite, adorned with satin drapery and sashes, with a chandelier, as bright as a starry night, twinkling overhead. In that room a young woman moved about, trailed by a coterie of young girls, attending her every wish.

Elizabeth.

A family friend since childhood, now soon to be wed to Victor Frankenstein. What did she know of his forays into the dark sciences, I wondered. Could he have dared tell her of his horrible creation? And if she were soon to be married to the man who gave me life, my father, then what did that make her to me?

Suddenly a noise from behind me. A shattered, disembodied voice.

". . . beth . . ." Henry said, the word hard as stone in his mouth. As I looked at Henry, I harkened back to the pain I had to endure as I strained to teach a long dead larynx to form words. Did I sound more like Henry than I dared to admit? Was my voice as harsh and riddled with shards of broken glass as was his?

". . . beth . . ." he said again. The castle squatted atop a low hill, rocky, strewn with black boulders. We made our way upward. It was unsteady work, navigating the ravaged ground, trying to stay on our feet. The light in the window burned overhead like a beacon. Calling us forward.

For a moment I paused, put a hand out to stop Henry's progress, as well. I stared up at that magnificent window, watched the flurry of activity from within, the pretty white dresses of the bridal party swishing like circling swans, Elizabeth smiling—I could see her that clearly now; she was smiling—and then . . . the groom. He stood in the corner, watching the spectacle, like an observer removed from the actual event. He was smiling also.

". . . no see . . . bride . . ."

"She's there," I said. "Beautiful as the sun."

Henry waved a hand, angrily.

". . . no . . . no see bride . . . bad . . ."

I felt badly for not understanding him earlier. "Oh, yes. He is not supposed to see the bride before the wedding. You are right. But Victor Frankenstein, you may be assured, is not the type of man to be hand-tied by tradition."

We continued upward, minutes later reaching our goal. A large veranda swept out away from the window. We climbed the stone banister, cold as bone to the touch, and

236

clambered onto the enormous expanse of the veranda. A wind howled out of the south, carrying the rich scents of the Danube, the air thick with mist.

Victor Frankenstein stood, elegant in his black tuxedo, his slim face handsome and vital. He laughed as his future wife scurried about in the room, preparing, and trying, also, to shoo him away.

"Inappropriate, Victor," I could hear her say through the glass double doors leading from the balcony. "You know it is. Now please leave. If you don't I will scream."

But it was not Elizabeth who screamed.

It was Frankenstein.

His eyes had been drawn to the veranda. Almost inexorably. As if he had no choice other than to look out at the two shadowy figures standing there in the fog.

Victor dropped his wine goblet to the stone floor—it shattered violently, a thousand shards of glass tumbling along the floor like an explosion of diamonds—and began to howl, a horrible, twisted wailing, from the depth of his soul.

The girls of the bridal party turned toward the doors and filled the air with screaming of their own. Then, one by one, they ran from the room. Only Victor, his back to the corner, and Elizabeth, remained. She cowered against him, eyes wide. My father's face, once flush with terror, began to change. To harden, jaw tightening, as horror turned to anger. He thrust Elizabeth aside, almost as if she had in some way transgressed against him.

"... Victor ... please ... what is it? Who are these men? What do they want?"

"NO!" Frankenstein's voice was ragged with fear. And loathing. "Not you. Not you."

It had been more than two years since last I saw him, and yet the pain of his rejection still stung me deeply. More pain than I could ever imagine, and I cursed myself for it. Why did I so need this man's approval? Why did his dismissals brutalize me so?

I suppose I felt that in the years we had been separated he perhaps would have regained some of his senses. That he would have reconsidered his response to me. That he would not shun me again.

"It cannot be you. No. No." He fell back against the far wall as if pushed, and then, as I followed his line of vision, I could see that it was not I who had brought the hateful, wrathful outcry from him, after all.

It was Henry.

"... this time ... Victor ... I will not go ... so easy ..."

Henry pulled open the double doors, warmth from the fire inside the room roiling out and prickling my flesh. I laid a hand upon Henry's right sleeve, just above the elbow, hard. Beneath his coat, I could feel the urgent tug of his muscles.

"Henry, what is it? What has you so upset?"

And indeed, Henry Clerval was agitated beyond any reasonable explanation. His eyes stark, mouth twisted into a near snarl.

"Henry," I pleaded, "Tell me."

He told me nothing, but, as fate would have it, he did not need to. For Victor Frankenstein would unknowingly and unthinkingly provide the explanation for the events of the evening when next he spoke.

"It can't be you," he repeated, desperate. "It can't. I watched you die. I felt you die. Felt it ebb away beneath my own hands."

Elizabeth landed on the stone floor with a dull thud, blood beading on her forehead. She did not move, fainted dead away.

My God, I thought. Could it be true? Henry Clerval's murderer was . . . Victor Frankenstein?

Henry said nothing more. Instead he charged, in a blind fury, roaring. Father screamed, helpless, pushing his back against the wall as if trying to break through it. Henry grabbed him around the neck, squeezed, his teeth gritted in rage.

I ran to the two men, intent on separating them, no matter the pain to myself. I could not let Henry snap his neck, not like this, in cold blood, without learning of the whole story. But before I could reach them, Henry released his grip. Victor Frankenstein stood gasping, hand to his throat. Henry stood beside him. Smiling.

". . . have you looked yet?" Henry said.

Father did not answer. By the look of the welts around his windpipe, he could not answer.

". . . have you?" Henry roared, impatient.

Father shot upright, spittle forming in the corners of his mouth. "What is it? What do you want to know? Tell me before I dash your brains against the floor. This time making sure you are dead. Dead."

". . . the little one . . . so sweet . . . have you looked for him . . .?"

"What the devil are you talking about?" Victor croaked.

". . . William . . . that is his name, is it not? . . . William . . . so sweet . . ."

Father's face turned ashen, drained of color. "William? What of him? What business is my little brother of yours?"

Again, Henry smiled, his eyes dark and malign. ". . . have you looked for him lately . . .?"

Father fought to look strong, to cobble together some semblance of composure. But it was futile. "My, God. If you have harmed him I will . . ."

Henry reached in his front pocket, his movements already beginning to demonstrate a fluidity and grace that have forever eluded me. He pulled out a small locket, dangling from a gold chain. He threw it to my father. Eyes cast toward the floor, he never attempted to catch it. Instead he watched as it skittered noisily along the stone floor before coming to a stop in the corner. He closed his eyes and began to weep.

It was certain that he recognized the keepsake, and he knew what it must mean that Henry now had it in his possession. And I, feeling betrayed, heartsick, realized to where Henry had disappeared last night in the woods. He had not simply gotten lost; he had gone hunting. For a little boy. For vengeance against the man who murdered him.

". . . he did not suffer . . . much . . ."

Father screamed. Arms flailing, he charged Henry, but his actions were of no consequence. Henry easily batted him away.

Father fell to the floor, blood creeping from a small gash above his lip. "Dear God, why? How? How could you be here in front of me? Surely I must be seized with some terrible fever, or racked by a nightmare I cannot escape. Yes, that's it. I am sleeping, soundly, enshrouded in a nightmare. For what else could it be? I killed you. With my bare hands. For your betrayal . . . you and Elizabeth. I know it was your doing. She would never have consented to such sordid behavior had you not held sway over her. She loves me . . . only me. The two of you . . . that was a mistake. She knows that . . ."

His words trailed away. And with them any hope that I would ever gain grace with my father. Henry Clerval, who I had known only as Victor Frankenstein's best friend, was much more. He was a philanderer and a cheat. He and Elizabeth? How could I have known such a thing?

Father, eyes rimmed purple with rage and hate, looked up. At me. Trembling. "This was your doing. Terrible, twisted beast. Monster. This was your revenge upon me? Bringing my hated nemesis, this traitorous wretch, back from the grave."

"No, no," I interjected. How could he think such a thing? He must know why I had done this. I did it for only one reason. Only one.

Because I loved him.

"Hound from hell! That is what you are. A beast coughed from the very bowels of the earth. I should never have tampered with realms outside the control of man. Never."

"I found your diaries . . . I read them . . . I thought if I . . ."

"Out. The both of you. Out. You do not belong here. My poor William. Poor little William. You beast."

". . . you are the reason we are here . . . Victor . . . this is your doing . . ." Henry crossed the room slowly. Father, fear springing sudden and dark back into his expression, scampered away. Henry lifted Elizabeth from the ground, softly. Passionately. ". . . we will go . . . as you wish . . . but first . . . one last kiss . . . from my beloved . . . Elizabeth . . ."

Henry pressed his lips delicately against those of the unconscious Elizabeth. She moaned quietly, but did not awaken. Henry held her close, then turned to Victor and smiled again.

There was sharp crack, like firewood popping in a hearth, as Henry snapped Elizabeth's frail white neck.

"Nooo," my father cried. Henry dropped the lifeless, beautiful Elizabeth to the ground. ". . . see you in hell, Victor Frankenstein . . ." he said as he turned, dashing for the double doors to the balcony.

I still stood transfixed, immobilized by shock and horror, when he crashed into me, shoulder to my chest, and knocked me to the ground.

". . . and you, as well . . ." he said to me. And then he was gone. Out the doors, leaping across the stone balustrade of the veranda and disappearing into the cool black fog beyond.

When I turned back, father was cradling his fiancé in his arms, tears leaving deep trails in his face. He looked up at me, black hatred filling him.

I had come here to gain my father's acceptance, but instead . . .

"I will track you to the ends of the earth. Know that in your heart, monster. I will follow you, hunt you, and when I find you I will send you back where you belong."

"But, father . . ."

"What," Victor screamed, face red, shaking as if experiencing a seizure. "What did you call me? What did you say, you Goddamned sick pathetic animal? Answer me!"

I looked at him for a moment. Saddened and shamed for what I had done, but also appalled at what he had become, as well.

"Nothing," I said.

Then, I too, jumped from the balcony and softly vanished into the thick forest of the night. Intent that in the morning I would begin my journey. To where, I was not yet certain. Only that it would be away from the eyes of man.

Forever.

INTO DARKNESS.

SEVERAL HOURS had passed since Victor began his story. It had grown even colder, the night air sharp as a blade.

Jonas exhaled. Heavily. A cloud of white curling around his face.

He thought of the old adage: at a loss for words. Never had it held such forceful meaning to him as it did now. What was there he could say?

He looked at the man beside him. And that is exactly what he was; a *man*. Compassionate. Sensitive.

And lonely.

He certainly was no monster.

Jonas had read Shelley's account of Dr. Frankenstein a number of times before leaving on his journey. Several times straight through; other times reading only selected passages. He knew much of it was simple folklore, and utterly inaccurate, but he could never have guessed at how bizarre and twisted the true tale really was.

Victor shifted, and then rose to his feet. Jonas attempted to do the same, but instead only grunted. His legs were asleep. Victor, looming over him, the full moon peering over one shoulder like the wide open eye of God, reached out a gloved hand. Jonas took it, and was quickly on his feet, as well.

"So you had every intention of coming back with me," Jonas said. "I never had to convince you."

Victor smiled. It was the first time Jonas had ever seen him do so. "That's why I didn't kill you earlier tonight." Then, as quickly as it had appeared, the smile vanished. Victor's face was awash again in solemnity and pain. "I made my way north, almost entirely by foot, to the coast, where I was able to smuggle myself aboard a steamer headed for the North Pole. As in Shelley's telling, my father did eventually find me, though how I still have no idea. But by the time he came to me, he was quite mad, speaking in clipped sentences, rocking himself to sleep at night hugging his knees to his chest. He was able to tell me only one thing I understood clearly: He said there was another diary. More notes concerning the creation of life. The first diary was incomplete, and likewise, the second. But together . . . together they could help future generations unlock the secrets of life and death. I possessed the first journal, and of the other, I could surmise whose hands it had fallen into. Henry Clerval . . . Lucias Angel. That is why he seeks me, why he sent you.

And, I as well, seek information from him. I must find the other journal, and once and for all, dispose of the wickedness Baron Von Frankenstein unleashed onto this world."

"You will destroy them both?" Jonas said.

"Forever. There are many things better left undiscovered, many truths better left hidden."

"What happened to him?" Jonas said quietly. "To Victor, your father?"

"He died in my arms. By the time he found me, his madness had surpassed his quest for revenge. In the end, I am not even certain he was aware of who I was, or that he was responsible for bringing me into this world."

Jonas hugged himself, patting his arms briskly. "How long before Angel finds us?"

"He has a very dedicated cabal of sycophants ready to do his bidding. In all the years I have been away, so much has not changed. The vainglorious quest for wealth. And power. And the level that those surrounding the wealthy will stoop to do their dirty work. I'm sure the streets are flooded now, even as we speak, with Angel's minions. Turning over every rock. We should warn Shaye. They will come for him first looking for information."

"What about my friend? Walton? I can't leave him with Angel. He will kill him. Brutally."

"Yes, or worse."

"So what do you suggest we do?"

Victor took a few tentative steps away from Jonas, age-old joints popping, cartilage creaking like leather.

"Perhaps we should not allow Lucias to find us. To track us down like animals. Instead, perhaps we should bring the fight to him."

"Go to him? What are you talking about? *Who* should go to him?"

Victor turned into the bitter wind, and said over his shoulder, "All of us."

FAMILY MAN.

AT TIMES, even as a man pursues a course he knows is folly, he finds that he cannot stop himself. With a thick heart, pushing ice water through his veins, he continues forward, imagining that his foolishness will yield beauty and understanding.

Yet, Cooper Shaye wondered, how often does that happen.

She will faint. Or lash out at him. Or scream, as she had done before. There was no way this could end well; he knew that. But . . .

. . . he trudged onward, into the ravenous teeth of winter, back hunched against the cold.

He had not been able to dislodge the image of her from his mind, not since that day outside Water Tower, the crowds pushing in on all sides, her face slackening at the sight of him. She had looked so beautiful. So . . . *alive*.

The whiteness of her skin. The long-ago smile.

Cooper stopped along Clark Street, just south of Diversey, in front of a building that had once housed his favorite used bookstore. Dusty volumes stacked to the ceiling. Now the windows were soaped over, the front doors boarded closed.

As he continued north he thought of his two young children. One of Cooper's biggest regrets was that he had no pictures of Benjamin and Lilly, no way of keeping their faces fresh in his mind. And what must they look like now? Lilly was an infant when he died, now . . . now she would be walking, saying her first full sentences. She would be more than two years old.

And Benjamin, who had just turned five the last time Cooper had seen him, would be seven now. Strong and handsome. But would either recognize him? Surely, Lilly would not. She had never really known him. Most of the time he had spent with his young daughter, he had himself been in a hospital bed. The cancer marching almost unimpeded through him.

But Benjamin, that was a different story. He would remember. The walks in the park. The ball games. Wrestling on the floor before dinner, Jennifer warning that someone was going to get hurt. The bedtime stories.

He would remember all of that. He was sure of it.

Cooper Shaye caught a sudden ghost-thin flash. He turned his head. And saw . . . himself. Reflected in the window of a greasy diner. He was filthy. His tattered raincoat dripping from his willowy frame. Plain blue cap, darkened with foulness. With a bony hand he pulled aside the front flap of the raincoat. Beneath, a grimy sweatshirt, the magic kingdom emblazoned across the front, standing in relief against Cinderella's famous castle. Disney World. They had taken Benjamin right before Jennifer became pregnant with Lilly. Cooper smiled wide, recalling the wide-eyed glare of wonder that had crossed his son's face so many times that day. First during the Pirates of the Caribbean (which they had ridden three times), then at the Jungle Cruise, and then, most spectacularly, during the electric parade that took place just past nightfall. Float after float, incandescent, burning a million colors in the soft darkness of the Florida night, pushed past them. Benjamin sat atop his father's shoulders, eyes pinwheeling.

Christ, what would they think of him now? Dirty, stained, crumpled. And what of the shock? What would they do when they saw him again? Would he be able to comfort Jennifer, to calm her down long enough to tell her his story?

Cooper Shaye had laid out a plan he knew to be the right one. He was going to walk into that fire, with the others, and leave this earth behind, as God had intended. He was going to end the pain and suffering, for all of them.

But what if he still had a chance at spending time with his children again, with his beloved Jennifer? It could never be as it was, he knew that, but why couldn't it work? Why couldn't he see his wife's crooked smile again, and watch his children grow?

Why?

At Diversey Avenue, Cooper stopped, pulled himself against the darkened front window of a Starbucks, and watched the slow crawl of late-night traffic. The street was dotted with a few slow-moving cars, but not many. There were even less people. Homeless stragglers, ragged and hump-shouldered.

A bitter swell of nostalgia and longing tugged at him as he looked toward the Far East restaurant on the opposite side of the street. It was there Jennifer had told him she was pregnant with Benjamin. Cooper had eaten the rest of the meal smiling, his body numb with the news.

Everywhere he looked now, more memories floated to the surface, flickering like dark shadow plays. Places where they had shopped, where they had eaten, and played, and walked, talked, kissed, held hands.

Cooper rubbed his eyes, hard, purple starbursts firing off in his head. For now, he had to put the memories aside, let them sink back into the darkness of his subconscious. He had to stay focused.

He crossed the street without waiting for the light. It immediately darkened as he left the bright overhead lamps of Diversey and settled into the quiet, tree-lined neighborhood he had once called home.

He walked east along Cottage, toward the lake, the wind twisting the bare branches of the trees into grotesqueries. Shadows skittering across the sidewalk. His breath caught in his throat. There it was . . . just ahead. A narrow six-flat, a small alley on one side, a quiet brownstone pressing in close on the other.

They lived in one of the two condos on the bottom floor. It had always made Cooper a bit leery to be at street level; the thought that people could sometimes look into their living space bothered him. But Jennifer loved the garden out front. And Cooper could not take that away from her.

Cooper squinted, searching for a light. But there were none. He had not expected any. It was late. Jennifer would have work in the morning. Benjamin would have school. Where did Lilly go during the day, Cooper wondered. Day care? Maybe to Jennifer's mother's?

Such sadness. To be away for so long. To have missed so much of their childhoods.

Cooper Shaye hugged the shadows as he made his way to 171 East Cottage Avenue. The garden in front was iced over, asleep for the winter. Cooper swung his legs over the small, wrought iron fence that circled the tiny yard and made his way to the back.

Cooper stopped, wiped his forehead, stared up at a small darkened window. He felt that his heart should be racing, pumping him full of warmth . . . but nothing. The window seemed to stare back at him, only blind, dead.

Suddenly, a ringing. Startled, Cooper faded back into the shadows. Then the window came to life, flush with warm yellow light. It was a phone, still ringing, still ringing. Then it stopped and Cooper could just make out a mumbled voice from within. Jennifer; it had to be her.

Another light clicked to life, this one in the living room. Cooper followed it, edging along the side of the building.

He peered around the corner, sticking his head out just far enough to see into the front bay window.

There she was. Cooper felt weak. She stood by the door, a girl in her arms, half asleep. My God, Cooper thought, could that be Lilly? My baby girl? She's so big.

Then a bedroom door swung open and out walked a young boy. Handsome, slim, hair tussled from sleep. Benjamin. He put his arms around Jennifer's waist and she pulled him in tight around her.

And there they stood. His family. As if awaiting his return. Cooper had second-guessed coming here. Had done so over and over again. But he had to come back. He couldn't go on any longer without them.

So now what? Should he ring the buzzer? Or maybe wait until morning? Perhaps try to catch Jennifer on her way to work, explain everything to her. The pain and the suffering. Then they could tell the kids.

A family again.

Cooper had little time to play out the possibilities in his head. A violent white splash of light interrupted his thought as a pair of headlights washed over the front of the building. He flattened himself out against the wall.

A taxi pulled up alongside the curb and out stepped a man, business suit, leather briefcase and overnight bag. He paid the driver and half ran to the front foyer of the building. Cooper struggled to make sense of what he saw, of what was happening. He hoped this man was not carrying with him bad news. First the phone call at this late hour, then the kids waking up. Then this.

Cooper returned to the front bay window, staring in, a ghost in the night.

Inside, Benjamin hopped on one foot, excited, smiling. Cooper felt relieved. Everything was fine. Just fine.

Then the front door swung wide . . . and in walked the man. Tall and lean. Almost elegant. Benjamin jumped into his arms, kissed him on the cheek. Then, he leaned down and Jennifer kissed him on the cheek, as well.

Cooper faltered, like he had been punched in the stomach. Disoriented and off balance. Then, Lilly—little, beautiful Lilly, with her blonde curls and dimpled cheeks—reached out for the man, nearly falling out of Jennifer's arms as she lunged into his waiting grasp. The man hugged her tight, kissed her, hugged her again.

Then the little girl spoke. Just one word. In a strong but innocent voice. Cooper fell to his knees, the strength drained from him. He brought his hands to his face, quickly. It was an unconscious reaction, one ingrained into him. He wanted to cry—needed to cry—and so, without thought, his hands shot to his face to wipe away the tears. But of course, no tears came. Tears were for the living.

Then the little voice again. Sweet and quiet, yet like a nail into Cooper Shaye's heart. She said just one word again. Just one.

Voice filled with happiness, hugging the strong man in the doorway, she said, "Daddy."

TO THE GROUND.

JONAS PULLED THE COLLAR OF HIS COAT up around his ears and cinched it tight with his balled fist.

Walking west, through neighborhoods of decay and desperation, the beauty of Chicago's lakefront seemed a million miles away. Corner liquor stores, bars encasing the windows, dotted every city block, nearly caving in upon themselves from neglect. The darkness of night pressed in on every side and Jonas could see shuffling figures at the periphery of his vision. Figures he was certain would be making their way toward him now had it not been for Victor by his side.

And the hundred undead shambling along behind him, following him blindly.

"Before we do anything else," Jonas had told Shaye before their journey had begun here tonight, "there is unfinished business we have to attend to. The laboratory where the Bone Welder experimented on Victor . . . it's still running. And as long as it is, they will bring more people there. And more. Trying to unlock their terrible secrets. My oldest friend in the world is being held captive there. Because of his connection to me."

Shaye had simply nodded. "Tell us when it is time to go."

A silver moon hung crooked and alone high above them, sinking the undead all around Jonas now into stark relief. They moved in unison, a single mind. Crushing in upon each other.

In the distance, at the end of the next block, Jonas could see the dark house huddled along a row of abandoned buildings. Its front porch caved in on one side, its windows covered with plywood, its roof slanting like a listing ship. The house—the entire neighborhood—was drenched in despair. Jonas could feel it to his very bones. A prison without walls. A jail in which every occupant had already been dealt a life sentence.

"You have a plan?" Cooper Shaye asked, suddenly at his side.

"Get my friend out. Shut this place down. Forever."

"And you don't think we're going to be met with any resistance? After you broke Victor out, they must have upped the security."

"That's why we brought all of them along," Jonas said, sweeping his arm toward the stumbling horde of the undead. The Hidden. "Strength in numbers."

"You know that in a confrontation, they are not going to be a great deal of help to you."

"Yes, Shaye. I know full well about their . . . limitations. Let's just hope the occupants of this house aren't as equally enlightened."

Up ahead there was movement. Jonas stopped, holding out his hand, halting Victor's progress and Shaye just behind him.

"What is it?" Victor said, his voice as dark as the surrounding night.

"I saw something," said Jonas. "Coming out of the house."

They all stared ahead, into the gloom of Chicago's forgotten side of town. One lone streetlamp burned high above the corner. Instead of shedding a safety net of light, as it was surely intended to do, its cancerous glow threw the crooked porch steps and cavernous sidewalk cracks and abandoned cars into absurd, carnival shadows.

The movement from within the house caught Jonas's eye again. And then, a figure emerged, moving stealthily, trying not to draw attention. Even from this distance, Jonas could see it was a man. Tall, with eyeglasses that winked in the milky glow of the streetlamp.

When the man turned toward them, he froze, his fingers splayed out before him like talons.

"This is not a good development," Victor said.

"You know him?" Jonas asked.

"Name is Page. He's one of the men who . . . works with Lucias."

"He's the one that cut into you?" Jonas said. "That sliced you apart?"

"One of them. But he's not the one who enjoyed it. He actually offered me a kindness. The only person in this terrible place to do so."

Victor rubbed his right arm, along the suture lines where Dr. Page had reattached the appendage.

Page stood in the jaundiced pool of light, unmoving. He looked to Jonas like he was transfixed. Frozen.

But then, wordlessly, as if trying to draw minimal attention to himself, he began to move his arms.

"What the hell is he doing?" Shaye said. "Is he . . . *waving?*"

"Maybe he wants to make up and be friends," Jonas said.

Victor's eyes narrowed. "He is not waving," he said. "He's trying to tell us to stay in our place. To not come forward."

"So he's *shooing* us?"

Page was beginning to move his arms more frantically now, an agitation and aggression setting in. His mouth was moving, as well. He began to look over his shoulder, furtively, as if they were all apart of some great conspiracy.

"He's nervous," Shaye said.

The streets were eerily quiet, ghostly in their abandonment. No cars moved on the street at this late hour. And other than the flailing Dr. Page and some of the shadowy figures moving through the darkness just beyond their line of vision, there wasn't another soul within eyeshot.

It led Jonas to wonder if Angel hadn't paid to have this entire street secure, perhaps buying every single decrepit house in the neighborhood to help keep his terrible hidden laboratory even more steeped in shadow and mystery.

Page, now clearly bordering on frantic, picked up a discarded piece of plywood from the garbage-strewn front yard of the house and then searched the ground until he came away with something shiny. A nail perhaps, thought Jonas. Then he scratched violently onto the piece of wood and held it above his head.

"Just tell us what you want to tell us," Shaye shouted. "We can't see your damned sign from here."

Page's eyes went wide and he put his finger to his lips.

"Be quiet," Victor said. "He wants us to be quiet."

"And why the hell should we listen to someone who strapped you to a table and proceeded to cut into you like you were a lab rat?"

"He's up to something," Jonas answered. "And he doesn't want Angel's men inside the house to hear about it."

"Well, why don't we go beat it out of him," Shaye said. "I'm tired of this game."

Page was now in his hands and knees, scrambling through the detritus beside the shattered sidewalk. This time he came away with a roof shingle, one of many scattered throughout the yard. The nail began to move furiously again. This time when he held it up, the scratches glowed in starch relief against the black shingle.

It was but a single word:

BOOM

Jonas took a step backward. "Oh, Jesus," Jonas said. "Everyone move! Back. Back. We need to get back."

He began pushing the undead that were gathered around him, confused and frightened now by the urgency in his voice.

"You're scaring them," Shaye said.

"At the moment, I really don't care. Help me get them the hell out of here."

Victor put a gloved hand on Shaye's shoulder. "Do what he says, Cooper."

In the distance, they could see Page drop the shingle into the dead brown grass at his feet before dashing away into the stagnant night.

Jonas began to run, pushing the undead in front of them. Urging them on. Begging them to move faster.

"For God's sake. Everyone. Please. Hurry. Hurry!"

Victor and Shaye corralled the others, pulling them, pushing them. None of them understood a thing, but Victor and Shaye fought to comfort them. To tell them everything was going to be okay . . . but they had to keep moving.

They had to get as far away from this house as possible.

They had not even gotten a full city block when they heard it.

A thunderous roar. A demon unleashed from its chains. The ground shook, and Jonas lost his footing. He crashed to the ground. Sprawled on the cold concrete of the sidewalk, he craned his neck back toward the spot they had last seen Page. Where the house had been just moments ago, a fireball blossomed into the sky. Then another explosion. And another monstrous fireball, red as the sun, burning, crackling. Heat rushed out toward Jonas and the others, enveloping them. The fireballs climbed higher and higher, turned black around the edges, and then began to slowly dissipate in the dull wind.

Where Angel's laboratory once stood, there was now only rubble, scorched and aflame.

Jonas fought a dizzying spell of nausea. Closed his eyes. The world spun. When he opened his eyes again, nothing had changed. Chaos. And carnage.

Suddenly a gloved hand appeared. Jonas grabbed it firmly, and Victor pulled him to his feet. The heartsick wail of sirens roared in the far distance but they were moving closer, closer.

Plumes of smoke—gray, white, black—rolled from the site of the ruined building like storm clouds. A fine rain of soot drifted down and covered Jonas's shoulders and the top of his head like a gentle gray snowfall.

"We need to get out of here," Shaye said. "We do not want to be here when the police arrive."

Shaye pushed the undead even more urgently, cajoling them, mindless cattle being driven to an unknown fate.

But they listened to Shaye, much more so than they ever would Jonas. They trusted him implicitly, even if they didn't know why. And because of that, they were moving much faster, crossing through the dark midnight streets.

Jonas was left alone at the rear with Victor by his side. He turned back one last time toward the smoking ruins of the house, the smoke twisting toward the stars, a phalanx of red flames dancing amongst the carnage.

Jonas's heart felt as if it had seized in his chest, a motor that had been neglected of oil. A sadness washed over him so profound, he had to bite his lip to keep the tears forming in his eyes at bay.

"I'm sorry, Jonas," Victor said quietly toward the devastation. "About your friend. I'm so very sorry."

Jonas turned away from the burning ruins, his teeth clenched so tightly that his eyes hurt, and muttered quietly into the wind, "I tried, Walton. Forgive me, old friend, but I tried."

Then he followed the hordes of undead into the cold winter night.

SIMPLE.

KILL THEM ALL.

Bring Burke and The Monster back unharmed.

But kill the rest.

His orders were as simple as that.

No, not kill. That wasn't the right word. Because they were already dead. No, the word that Angel had used was 'eliminate.' That was it. Eliminate.

And Raymond Grimes planned to relish every minute of it. But thanks to the treachery of Dr. Page, he would have to add another person to his list.

What had the fool been thinking?

They had planned for weeks to shut down the West Side lab, like they did with sites all over the world from time to time, just to cover their tracks. Keep suspicious eyes from lingering on them for too long.

Grimes saw an opportunity to resolve two problems at once. Walton Wallace had never been anything more than a bargaining chip. A way to get Jonas Burke to come to *them*. And Grimes knew he would bring the others with him, the shambling undead that Grimes had grown to despise for their weakness. Their feeble-mindedness.

The explosives would take care of everything. Return Angel's slow-witted experiments to the dust from which they had come. Kill two birds with one stone. But for reasons Grimes could not even begin to fathom, Page had warned them away. When they were just seconds from stumbling blindly into the house. Grimes had imagined the smell of all that burning flesh. The screams. And it had made him happy beyond words.

But now . . .

He would certainly take care of Page in good time.

But first he had to track down the undead, as well as Jonas and the Monster.

It was best not to let the hatred he felt consume him. He must remain focused. For there was work to do.

Find them. Wipe them all out.

And bring back Burke and The Monster.

Simple.

Grimes fingered the knife in his front coat pocket, sharp as a dream.

WRITING ON THE WALL.

WHAT BOTHERED JONAS MOST was not the filth nor the dark nor even the danger.

It was the *noise*.

Like thunder crashing around him, the gods themselves hammering at his ears all night long.

"Do these infernal trains ever stop running?" Cooper Shaye said, his hands cupped over his ears, the skeletal framework of his fingers like some intricate latticework.

Union Station was the busiest in the city. There was not only the constant grind of the Metra commuter trains to contend with, but the long-distance Amtrak trains roared in all hours of the night and day as well. And in the warren of tunnels that wend beneath the station, where they now found themselves, the howl of the trains was amplified.

It was enough to drive a person crazy.

"Sadly, they do not," Jonas replied. "They are going to wreak havoc with your beauty sleep, which is a shame, because, brother, you could really use it."

"Come talk to me after you've been dead a year or two and tell me how well *you're* doing?"

Jonas knew they could not stay here for long. Despite the bantering, Shaye was right. If they remained here for long, they were going to come unmoored from their senses.

But the bombing at the laboratory left little doubt that Lucias had upped his campaign. He was in a full-scale battle to cover his tracks. And that was going to mean eliminating the ghosts of his past mistakes. His experiments were going to have to be eliminated.

Shaye felt strongly that their hiding place at The Lincoln Park Zoo was not compromised, that Lucias would never find them there. But seeing the lab go up in a moon-white explosion of light had convinced Jonas they would be better served by moving on. And Cooper Shaye did not argue.

Because everyone had heard the rumors. A strange undercurrent of fear was running through the streets of Chicago, particularly in the ragtag communities of the homeless.

The dark reality was that the homeless were vanishing from the streets. Victims of a campaign of cleansing they could never begin to understand. It was apparent that Lucias Angel was being indiscriminate in his manhunt. He had ordered his henchmen to erase the existence of any homeless person they came upon. Man or woman. Breather or otherwise.

The order couldn't be simpler. Just get rid of them.

Lucias's men were coming for them. Were coming for Jillian. And Jonas was not about to allow her to suffer any more at the hands of Lucias Angel.

High above, a train screamed into the station. A fine mist of dust trickled down covering Jonas in a gray sheen. Angel's failed and forgotten children—the Hidden— pressed in around him in the darkness. Jillian was out there, he knew. Among them. Her golden hair, once as lustrous as sunshine, now no more than straw. Hard and matted and as flat as her unfeeling eyes.

Several candles fluttered in the distance and in their blue, wavering shadows, Jonas could see the Hidden shifting in the pale light. Jonas choked on the feeling that he had failed them all in so many ways. He was protecting them now, with every bit of strength he could muster, so that he could turn around and watch Cooper Shaye lead them into their own blistering funeral pyre.

For a moment—a brief, perfect flash in time—there was silence. Jonas allowed the quietude to wash over him, pure as rain.

Jonas was unsurprised when a sudden scream ripped through the stagnant underground air. Another train, no doubt, its brakes squealing.

He waited for the fine mist of powder to shudder down. And waited.

But there was nothing.

Jonas sat up, heart thrumming. Maybe, he thought, maybe it hadn't been a train, after all. Maybe it was a different kind of scream entirely.

Suddenly a wave of the Hidden, sprawling and tripping over one another, was rushing toward him, knocking candles to the ground as they scrambled madly, their mouths stretched into violent, voiceless screams.

Cooper Shaye, his white face blanched with fear, was at his side. "What the hell is it? What are they doing?"

The Hidden stormed toward them, loping like stray dogs, terror burbling up in their throats.

"They're here," Jonas said. "They've found us."

Even in the dim light from the candles, Jonas could see the black figures in the distance, moving like shadows, the silver of their knife blades winking. Shaye was trying to corral the Hidden. Trying to control them and keep them moving with some semblance of order. But the screams continued and the silver blades soon turned dark. As Jonas saw the thickening coat of red forming on those blades, there could be no question that what he was looking at was blood. And that meant, terribly, there were Breathers down here with them, too. And they were getting cut down in the chaos.

Jonas felt an almost blinding surge of panic. "Come on, Shaye. Hurry. Get them the hell outta here."

More screams. And this time they were getting closer. So close that Jonas could *feel* the screams as well as hear them.

Lucias Angel's men raged against everything around them, swinging their bloodied knives, kicking and punching at anyone within reach. A Breather stumbled toward Jonas, mouth agape, hands on his throat, red rivulets of blood seeping between his fingers. The homeless man's mouth moved, gasping, perhaps trying to form words, but none came. He pitched forward onto his face, and lay still as stone.

Jonas waited until all the Hidden had run lurching by him, frantic with panic, and then followed close behind, acting as a buffer between them and Lucias's agents of terror.

A blaze of illumination erupted suddenly in the underground passageway, as a dozen flashlights burst to life. The milky beams of light swept across the terrified faces of the homeless, their eyes wide, jaws tight. The flat, emotionless faces of Angel's men were reflected in the lights they held in one hand, the dark blades in the other.

"Whach you all want?" Jonas heard someone say. "Leave us alone. We ain't done nothin' to you."

One of the men lurched forward, blade glinting, and whoever had spoken collapsed in a flurry of gurgling, gasping, panting. Jonas looked down at the concrete floor. A thick puddle of blood welled up against the side of his right shoe.

Jonas lashed out, a nearly electric hatred surging through him. His right fist smashed into the attacker's nose, cracking it loudly and sending him crumpled to the ground. The man writhed at Jonas's feet, hands cupped to his face, a trickle of blood wending its way through his fingers.

Jonas delivered a kick to the side of the man's head, in the soft crevice of his temple, that silenced him. Sprawled out before him, unconscious. Jonas reached for the man's blade.

"You do not have time to dole out retribution right now, Jonas," a voice warned beside him. "They will devour you. We must get out of here."

Cooper Shaye grabbed him by the wrist. Pulled him.

All the time, Jonas's blood bubbling madly in his veins. Hatred nearly consuming him. He wanted to do more than just stop these men. He wanted to *kill* them.

Angel's men were everywhere. A swarm of death and suffering. And they were nearly upon him. The Hidden that remained had already moved past him. The remaining Breathers had long since run screaming into the night air above.

Shaye was right. There was nothing to be gained from staying here. It was then that another voice materialized beside him, ghostly, as if disembodied.

Jonas turned to find a lean man leering at him, grinning through skeletal teeth, the flesh of his face peeling away in thin strips, like paint from a weathered barn.

"It's you," the man said. "The man who returned the Monster from the ice. Isn't that right?"

"If it's me you want, fine," Jonas spat at the man. "But leave the rest of these people alone. Let them be. They've done nothing to you. I'll come with you willingly if you just call these men off."

The man cocked his head, like a dog contemplating a whistle. "Where's the Monster? I need him, as well. Him and I . . . well, let us say that we have unfinished business."

My God, Jonas thought. *Victor. He hadn't seen him for hours.* A thin trickle of dread slipped slowly between his shoulder blades.

"I don't know where he is," Jonas said flatly.

The man pursed his lips, the flesh puckering like a wound. "Tsk. Tsk. What kind of keeper are you? And how about all your stumbling, bumbling companions with their rotted brains leaking out the side of their heads? Think they may know where the Monster is?"

The hollow, gunshot echo of a scream rattled the cavernous space. *The Hidden. What were Angel's men doing to those poor, lost souls?* "This does not involve them," Jonas said. "Take me to Angel. I'm not going to fight you. Just leave them alone."

The man smiled, but only the right side of his mouth moved. Jonas squinted into the gloom, noticing now for the first time the patchwork of flesh covering the man's face. An amateur mask sewn together with the skin of others. When the man grinned it became more pronounced. The skin of his lips parting slightly, the stitched flesh on his cheeks shifting out of place, like a child's puzzle just before it slides to the floor and dissolves into a thousand pieces.

"Bring them back. Kill the rest. Those were my directions."

Jonas did not fear this man, nor what Angel had in store for him. But he could not leave the Hidden down here alone and helpless. And certainly not Jillian, scrambling somewhere out in the stifling darkness, afraid. He could not leave her to meet this kind of an end.

Jonas turned and bolted into the darkness, toward the maelstrom of noise and screams of the Hidden falling like summer wheat before the scythes of Angel's men.

"Oh, good," the man called after him. "I was hoping you weren't going to make this too easy. I was so looking forward to a little bit of a *chase*."

The concrete was now sticky with blood beneath Jonas's feet as he ran.

Up ahead, flashlight beams careened into one another, a chaotic dance of light. Flashing. Swinging left to right. Floor to ceiling. A cavalcade of white luminescence.

And amidst the light—screams. Not only from the Hidden as they were falling beneath the meaty blades, but also the joyous screams of Angel's men, the bloodlust driving them into a blind frenzy.

Jonas ran into the maelstrom, unarmed and without any forethought. Suddenly faced with a stone-faced cadre of Angel's men, he realized the folly of his actions. A stocky man, his thick fingers wrapped around the base of a nightstick, charged at him. Jonas stopped him with an elbow across the bridge of his nose.

Two more men came at Jonas, this time more cautiously. Stalking him, moving side to side, sizing him up. Adrenaline burned through him like battery acid, every sense awakened by the danger he had thrown himself into. Yet, despite the scowling men now circling him, Jonas felt a strange current of relief. For, looking around, it was clear that the Hidden, somehow, had gotten away. Vanished as if into thin air.

They were nowhere to be seen. And Jonas knew the answer immediately.

Victor.

He had somehow ushered them to safety. Past the men with their winking blades. Past the crazed patchwork man with his melting face and proclamations to "kill them all."

He thought of Jillian. Hustled to safety, her soft memories perhaps warmed knowing that she had escaped harm.

Nearby, a yellowing light sprang warmly to life, as if one of Jonas's attackers had lit a gas lantern or even a torch. In the flickering light, Jonas caught a brief glimpse of one of the battered and timeworn walls of the underground passageway surrounding him. Amongst the chipped concrete and rusted struts, he could clearly see something else. Writing. Scratched rapidly into the surface of the concrete itself. A simple message.

We will be there to catch you when you fall

The message struck him for several reasons. Partly, without knowing exactly why, he felt the message was directed toward him. As if the message was meant for

Jonas and Jonas alone. Secondly, it was clear the message was very new, just recently scrawled furiously into the crumbling wall.

But Jonas had no idea what it could mean. And he simply had no time to give it any more thought.

Jonas, clearly distracted by the realizations that the Hidden were no longer in danger, still kept his eyes very much on the men closing in on him. He raised his fists, pulled his elbows in close to his body.

Despite his vigilance, there was simply no way he could see the dark shapes flickering past behind him. A ruffling in the darkness. But he felt the sharp pain behind his ear, and felt, too, the thin strand of blood that made its way along his hairline and then down his neck.

His eyes struggled to focus. But failed.

Jonas felt himself falling. Falling. (*We will be there to catch you when you fall*) Toward a floor that seemed a million miles away. Falling.

Then all was black.

CRAWLING TOWARD LIGHT.

THE FIRST CRYSTALLINE REALIZATION that he was still alive came when he heard the voices. He could not understand what was being said, but they were voices nonetheless.

He tried to sit up, but could not move. *Christ*, he moaned, *the pain*. Like a blowtorch at the base of his skull.

The voices continued, warbling incoherently. As if traveling through water.

Jonas opened his eyes. Flinched at the light. Closed them.

Somewhere, someone said, ". . . eees aaikk . . ."

He opened his eyes again. Slowly. He could feel his pupils contract as they struggled to focus.

What the hell had happened? He could remember the darkened warrens beneath the railway station, the trains rumbling overhead. The terrified Hidden scurrying like sewer rats before the gleeful brutality of Angel's hatchet men.

Men circling him. Toying with him, almost.

Yes, that was it . . .

. . . then nothing.

Blackness.

And what had become of Victor and Jillian and Shaye and all the Hidden?

Jonas tried again to sit upright. He realized now that it was not pain, nor disorientation, that prevented his movement. He was restrained. He could feel the leather straps around his wrists and ankles.

". . . eelin betta . . .?"

A man leaned over him. Then another. Jonas could not clearly make out their faces.

"Where am I?" Jonas asked.

One of the men laughed. "The end of the line," he said.

And then another voice. "No man should make the kinds of enemies you have, Mr. Burke. It's not healthy."

Jonas blinked. Heavily. His vision cleared, and he could see the two men now. They were both young—early twenties—with short, cropped hair. Dark. One wore glasses. The other, the taller of the two, had a tightly shaved goatee.

They both had the same eyes, Jonas noticed. Not the color. Not the shape. But the intensity. These were men who did what they were told, no matter, and who relished it.

"Mr. Angel has an offer," said Eye-Glasses.

"And anyone who knows anything—even a stupid son of a bitch like yourself—knows better than to refuse one of Mr. Angel's offers," said Goatee.

"He offers you a quick death."

"Very humane of him. You don't deserve it."

"You will never leave here, Mr. Burke. That should be clear to you by now."

"You are going to die."

"But there are many ways in which to die."

"Slowly."

"Painfully."

"The flesh pulled from your bones like so much wallpaper."

"Or quickly."

"Snap. It's over."

"Mr. Angel is giving you a choice."

The two men leaned back. Smiled.

"And what is it that I have to do?"

"Simple."

"Just tell us where they are."

"We searched the zoo."

"Nothing."

"Just old bones and mummified insects."

"We need to find them."

"Tell us and you are safe."

"Refuse and your screams will rattle these walls."

"One condition," Jonas said.

The two men stared, eyes as blank as the vacuum of space. "Yes," they urged impatiently.

"I tell no one except Angel himself."

One of the men laughed, a high, tinkling girlish laugh. "Silly, boy. Of course you'll be talking with Mr. Angel. He wouldn't have it any other way."

LAST STAND.

LUCIAS ANGEL, Jonas thought, was a man who straddled two worlds. He was clearly a man of the twenty-first century, sophisticated in appearance, well-heeled in political circles, on the cutting edge of technology the common masses would not be familiar with for decades.

And yet, looking around his enormous, towering home, Jonas could see that he was also a man with his feet still firmly planted in the nineteenth century.

On either side of Jonas, firm, strong hands cut into the flesh of his biceps. Eye-Glasses on one side and Goatee on the other. Neither spoke.

Which left Jonas to marvel at the Gothic gloom of Lucias Angel's estate, which in earlier times would simply have been called a castle.

Stone walls, gray, soared upward, impossibly high, the ceiling lost amid deep shadows. They journeyed through rooms that reminded Jonas of old English hunting lodges.

Wooden chandelier dangling from the arched ceiling. Monstrous Persian rugs—blood red, hunter green— thrown across the stone floors. Fire crackling in the hearth. A broad sword anchored above the fireplace, a great iron shield beside it, reflecting back the yellow glow of the many candles that lined the room.

They also passed through a great dining hall. An enormous mahogany table stretching from one end to the other, a white lace tablecloth draped over it, a vase containing an explosion of red roses in the middle. Then through a study. And another Great Room, replete with a suit of armor in the corner.

For a moment, Jonas felt a strange sense of vertigo. Like he was disconnected from the world he knew. Like he had traveled, unwillingly, back through time. That is until Goatee pulled gently on the visor of the suit of armor's helmet, and a hidden door slid silently open along the wall.

Yes, Lucias Angel was most definitely a man of two worlds. Ancient and modern. Obvious and hidden. Light and dark.

They stepped through the doorway. The door hissed closed behind them.

Before them stretched a long, curving passageway, lit only by gas lamps lining the walls. They could no longer stand three abreast, so the two flunkies pulled in behind him. One of them prodded Jonas in the small of the back with his knee. "Straight ahead," he growled. "Not a good idea to keep him waiting."

The passageway not only curved . . . it *rose* as well. Higher and higher. Like a spiral staircase. Jonas felt miles above the earth when the corridor abruptly—finally—ended.

And then, only a door.

Small. Carved from a rough, hard wood.

The two men behind Jonas coughed and cleared their throats. Even without seeing them, he could sense their nervousness.

There was no need to knock. The door opened on its own.

Jonas stepped into the room beyond, without being told to do so. It was not until the door slammed shut behind him that he realized he was alone. Eye-Glasses and Goatee were nowhere to be found.

The room was circular, rimmed with a semicircle of floor-to-ceiling windows. Through the towering windows, Jonas could see the diamond bright lights of the city. A fire crackled warmly in a stone fireplace. Bookshelves lined the opposite side of the room, the gold lettering on the spines of the leather-bound editions reflecting the orange flames of the fire.

In the middle of the room was a desk, thick and muscular, carved from wood as red as drying blood. A smattering of papers, neatly aligned, skated the edges of the desk and in its center, like a priceless museum piece on display, was a simple leather book. Hand-stitched. Worn with age.

A diary.

Jonas crossed quietly to the desk and flipped open the book, the pages as soft as goose down in his hands. He could feel the age in the paper, the brittle passage of time. He read the first page, skimming it breathlessly, electrified by what he saw there before him on the browning paper. He was already on the third page before he realized he was not alone. As quietly as possible he closed the slim volume.

The room was empty. And yet . . . it wasn't. Jonas Burke could see no one. But there was a presence. Strong and distinct. Even before turning around he knew that Lucias Angel was standing there. Watching him.

"Have you ever seen it from the lake?" Lucias's voice was sinewy and deep, yet somehow soothing. Fatherly.

Jonas felt a hand upon his shoulder as Lucias walked slowly past, never turning to look at Jonas. At the windows he stopped, hands folded behind his back, staring out into the darkness beyond. He wore a dark suit, so black he was nearly invisible in the dim light.

"It's an incredible sight," he continued. "Perhaps the most beautiful skyline in the world. Were you born here, Mr. Burke?"

"Yes."

Lucias Angel turned from the window. High cheekbones cut deep shadows into his face. And his eyes . . . to Jonas they looked as if they glowed. Amber red, burning, burning.

What is it they say about a man's eyes? Jonas tried to remember. That they are the windows to his soul? Yes, that was it. But what if the man had no soul? Then what?

What had those eyes seen over the years, Jonas wondered. Pain beyond reason. Terror and fear and horrors unspeakable. But was there more? Love, perhaps? Compassion?

That much Jonas could not tell—could *never* tell. Because that is what Lucias Angel's eyes bespoke of most. Secrets. Deep, dark and impenetrable.

"What is it you are thinking about?" the dark man asked. "Are you afraid that I am going to kill you now?"

"I've learned enough about death in the past few months. Perhaps it is something I should no longer fear."

A low, throaty chuckle. "Yes. There are worse things, aren't there? Tell me, has there been any change in your daughter?"

Jonas shook his head.

"Shame. It is not as I planned. Not at all. But nothing ever has been, I suppose."

"Aren't you going to ask me where you can find them?"

A smile. Weak. "Don't you think I could have discovered that answer by now had I really wished? But let me ask you—would you have told me had I asked?"

Jonas shook his head again. Stood silently. Waited.

Waited for a flash of anger, for this dark immortal to lash out at him. But that was not to be.

Lucias did not move. Only stared. The blackness in his eyes telling nothing. Then, catlike, graceful, he stepped away from the window. He waved Jonas forward. "Here. They've come."

Jonas walked slowly toward the window, and as he did a faint noise reached his ears. A distant murmuring. A rhythmic rumble of voices.

"See for yourself. This is why I had no need to ask you. I needn't have searched for my little lost darlings. They have found me instead."

Jonas peered out the window, down to the huge courtyard below. A white gravel driveway looped tightly around a marble fountain. A green expanse of lawn stretched to a low, stone barrier that outlined the estate's grounds. And scattered across the lawn, hundreds of tattered, moaning, staggering, blank-eyed creatures.

The Hidden.

The iron gate at the far end of the driveway was agape, forced open by the throngs of living dead that still choked through.

Somewhere down there was his daughter, Jonas thought. And at the front would be Victor. And Cooper Shaye.

The din was now overwhelming. A chorus of pain and confusion as the voices of the Hidden curled along the currents of Chicago's winter winds.

"You knew they were coming," Jonas said flatly.

"Of course. I knew Victor had not traveled all this way to stand idly by. He always was such a moral creature. And the rest of them . . . well, they have every right to seek me out, I suppose."

"Then why bring me here? The men downstairs . . ."

"They are hired hands. They know nothing of my true intentions. If I wanted you dead, I could have accomplished that with little effort. I brought you here because I knew they would follow."

Jonas cursed under his breath. "A trap."

Lucias laughed blackly. "Which, I suppose, makes you the bait."

Jonas angled back toward the door, trying to keep as much room between him and Lucias Angel as possible. "So now what? Kill them all? Wipe the slate clean?"

"You know perhaps more than anyone, Jonas, that I cannot kill them. Because they are, sadly, not alive. They are failed experiments. Eliminating them is not murder. It is nothing more than wiping clean the Petri dish so that we may begin anew."

"You were a man once, Henry. A good man. There is no reason to go on with this. To cause so much more pain. So much anguish."

Lucias turned away from the window, the city lights cutting him into a darkened silhouette, sharp as a diamond. "You are going to lecture *me* on pain?"

"As someone who has lost the only two people I have ever loved, I think I have the right."

Lucias bowed his head, as if ready to concede the argument.

"I tried to bring her back to you, Jonas. I did not do so to cause you more grief. Truly I did not. I meant only to bring life to the dead. Like men of science have struggled with for centuries."

"Then, as a man of science, I implore you to stop. This has all been a mistake. Have you not learned that death is what gives life meaning? For what else can make us savor each day, to strive to do our best, then the dark spectre of the Reaper hanging over us. Our time here is meant to be finite, Lucias, so that we do not take a single moment for granted."

Lucias smiled. "Ahh. I believe we have left the realm of science and entered into the rarified air of philosophy. I think in that regard you may have me at a disadvantage. My simple contention is this. It is better to be alive than to be dead. Wouldn't you agree?"

Lucias stepped toward Jonas, hands at his side, wearing a smile as dangerous as an oil slick.

Jonas edged even closer to the door. He knew there was no way he would reach it in time, just as he knew that Lucias planned to kill him on the spot. Jonas's usefulness to the man had run out.

But Jonas was beginning to form another plan in his head. Distant words played against the shadowy screen of his memory.

We will be there to catch you when you fall

Suddenly, an intercom mounted to the room's far wall squawked to life. ". . . Mr. Angel . . . have a serious problem down here . . . very serious . . . think you had better come at once . . . need to institute evacuation procedures immed . . ."

It was then that Jonas began to see the flames.

Outside, through the yawning floor-to-ceiling windows, the tranquil, dark beauty of hundreds of flicking torches drew nearer.

"Looks like the villagers have shown up," Jonas said, "and this time it is you who's the monster."

Angel turned toward the windows, pressed in close to the cold glass. "Mindless fools."

"And maybe I wasn't bait after all. Perhaps a better word would be decoy."

Angel stood motionless before the seamless pane of glass, seemingly transfixed by the teeming swirl of humanity below. As if he had not heard the urgent pleadings from the intercom.

Squawk. ". . . sir, please . . . they have breached the main gate . . . are at the door . . . don't know how much longer . . . oh, God . . . fire . . . surrounded . . . fire . . ."

The windows began suddenly to glow orange, a somber reflection of the flames that were right now beginning to consume Angel's mansion. When Lucias Angel turned away from the window and back toward Jonas again, his face had lost much of its elegance. Anger had slackened the tightness of his features; rage shaded his eyes to a pitiless black. For the first time, Lucias Angel looked to Jonas like someone—some*thing*—that had returned from the grave.

"If you were hoping to make a play for the door, Jonas, this is your chance. I'm not feeling particularly charitable right now, but I will give you the chance. Just for a second. Then I will rip your throat out."

"I had another idea," Jonas said, a voice playing over and over in his head, roaring like the surge of the ocean.

We will be there to catch you when you fall

when you fall . . .

"The door seems so . . . predictable," Jonas said. "And surely you are a man who likes surprises. But know this, Lucias, I will never let this go. I will never tire. I will never quit. I will track you to the ends of the earth. I'll devote my life to stopping you. And I'll do it in my daughter's name."

Jonas made a subtle nod toward the door, an almost imperceptible movement, little more than the flutter of a hummingbird's wings. But Lucias was ready, coiled. He lunged for him.

And in that moment, Jonas knew his ploy had worked. That he had led Lucias just enough to follow through on his real intentions. As Lucias charged at him, Jonas pivoted, changed direction and dashed *away* from the door. As fast as he could.

Toward the gleaming bank of windows.

And all the while, those words kept ringing in his ears.

We will be there to catch you when you fall

Right up until the moment a thundering shower of glass began to rain down upon him.

FALLING.

THE WINTER AIR CUT JONAS like a blade as he fell.

The orange glow of the flames climbing the walls of Lucias's home flickered in the corner of his peripheral vision, and outside the circle of fire, flooding the great expansive lawn of the estate, Jonas could see the Hidden. A veritable sea of ravished humanity. Pushing, clawing, moaning.

Their voices coiled like rusted springs.

And they were waiting for him.

We will be there to catch you when you fall

Waiting.

KEEPSAKE.

VICTOR REACHED OUT WITH A GLOVED HAND and pulled Jonas to his feet. "The front door wasn't an option?" he said.

Jonas shook crystallized shards of glass from his hair, brushed the powdery residue from his pants and sleeves. A razor-thin slash cut across the palm of one hand and his shoulder throbbed mercilessly, as if it had been separated, but considering the height of the fall, he could expect to feel no better.

As he was pulled from the ground, he looked back toward the frozen earth and the Hidden that were splayed there, bent and crumpled. Slowly, they rose to their feet, their faces blank.

Had they not been there to break his fall, Jonas was certain he would be dealing with much more right now than a sore shoulder.

The flames were spreading and had now engulfed the entire base of the mansion, searing the stone black in its wake. They climbed upward, as voracious as any animal, the blaze roaring and gnashing and turning the winter air feverish.

Jonas could hear a siren in the distance. They would never make it in time. They could set up their hook and ladders and spray a million gallons of water on the house, there was no way to stop this inferno at this point, Jonas knew.

The flames—deep red at the bottom, searing white near the top—were hypnotizing. Jonas watched them leap and dance. Waver and flicker.

The Hidden were doing the same. Their angry cries had subsided, their painful, defiant moans faded to silence beneath the jet-engine roar of the fire. Now they only watched.

Blank-eyed. Shoulders stooped. They stared at the fire. And stared.

Jonas let his gaze rise with the flames. Higher. Higher. Then . . .

. . . at the summit of the massive estate, just below the darkened eaves, his eyes came to rest on a window. And in that window, a shadowy figure. Standing still as time.

Jonas turned to see Victor craning his neck skyward, his gaze unwavering.

Victor stared as if trying to see across a universe, an infinite sea of space. The figure in the window shifted, and

Jonas was sure that Lucias Angel was staring back as well.
At his father. His creator.

Then he was gone. The window empty.

"What did you say to him?" Victor asked.

"That I'm looking forward to the next time we meet."

Victor turned back toward Jonas, his eyes distant. Jonas
could feel his pain, it hung between the two men, palpable
and real. A dark cloud of longing and regret.

Jonas reached into his inside coat pocket and pulled out
a slim leather volume.

A diary.

He handed it to Victor.

A gloved hand tentatively reached for it.

"What's this?"

"It's the reason Lucias wants that first journal so badly.
This one, I'm afraid, does not contain much scientific
merit. It's more . . . personal, I guess you could say."

"And Lucias let you have it?"

"Let's just call it loan. I'll be happy to return it to him.
Right down his throat. But I wanted you to see it first."

Victor pushed it back to Jonas.

"What could there be in this journal, Jonas, besides
more pain. Perhaps it's best that it remains a mystery."

Jonas, the skin on the back of his hands prickling from
the fire, gently nudged the decades-old journal back
toward Victor. "Just the first entry, Victor. That's all you
need to see."

Victor, the deep, black pain Jonas had become accustomed to creeping into his eyes, flipped the book open.

And he read.

THE CREATOR SPEAKS.

THERE HAVE BEEN MANY who have labeled me a heretic, others simply a fool. As a man of science I have achieved what no other before me has: The creation of life. Formed from the remnants of the dead, sewn together and jolted to life through electricity and alchemy.

But as a man I have failed.

For I did much more than simply create life. I created a human. Yet I did not treat him as such. I shunned him, turned from him as if he were an animal. A disgrace. And in my response to him I now realize my own failing.

I see now it was my attempt at perfection that was my greatest folly. For whom among us is perfect? Is not imperfection the quality that makes us human?

He wanted only what each of us crave. Companionship. Understanding. Love. But I was too consumed with madness at the time to share anything but hatred for him. He was not a monster when I created him, but if he became one, certainly it was from the inhuman treatment I extended toward him.

Perhaps in focusing solely on the creation of life, I disregarded and misunderstood what it is to be truly alive.

To be alive is more than a physical phenomenon. More than a mere medical condition. It is a spiritual quest.

To be alive is to be human.

And how do all of us, poor lost souls that we are, achieve our humanity? How do we go from selfish, insensitive children to concerned, impassioned adults?

Why, the answer is simple. We learn from our parents.

Certainly those who referred to me as a fool in the past will think my next actions quite mad. But what choice do I have? I can no longer live with the mistakes I have made and I most certainly cannot expect my child to live with them either.

And so I will seek him. Travel to the ends of the known world if I must. For before I die, I must look into his lost gray eyes and tell him what I was not man enough to tell him when he drew his first breath.

That he is my child. My son. And that I love him.

Only then will I be able to say I have truly created life. When I can look at my son and tell him that he is good. That he is noble. And that, no matter what torment he must endure in this world, I will always be his father.

DUST TO DUST.

VICTOR QUIETLY CLAPPED THE JOURNAL SHUT, a solemnity as deep as the grave surrounding him.

"That's why he followed you to the North Pole," Jonas said. "Madness had consumed him by the time he reached you, but . . . now you know why he sought you. He did not seek you out to destroy you. He went looking for his son."

Victor clasped the journal tight against his chest. He closed his eyes. For long seconds, he remained motionless. Then he opened his eyes, moist and red. "Thank you," he said.

Suddenly, off in the cold distance, the sound of the screeching sirens drew nearer.

Jonas frowned. "We had better get everyone out of here. The firemen and police will have a lot of questions we probably don't want to answer."

Victor stopped. Turned his head. "Jonas, I thought you knew."

"What?"

"That we are not going back. Not to the zoo, or lower Wacker, or the train station. We are staying here."

Jonas could feel the flames warming his back. "Oh my God. Jesus, Victor . . . the fire . . .?"

"Too much suffering, Jonas. It is time. This world does not want us. Nor do we want it."

"But surely . . . there's some other way."

"Perhaps you will tell me then. What is it we should do? What other torment would you have us endure? You have known this day was coming for some time, Jonas."

Jonas fought with a thousand different responses, a thousand different reasons why Victor should not do this. But he could not force himself to voice any of them. Because he knew them all to be false. The reason he did not want Victor to walk into the inferno, with the Hidden following behind, was simple: he did not want his daughter to be one of them.

He did not want to watch her die. Not again.

"All of them are going to go with you?"

"Yes. Everyone. Including her."

Jonas looked around the yard. At the white-eyed Hidden. So lost. So desperate for release from pain. "Can I speak with her first?"

"Jonas, I don't think . . ."

"Just for a minute. One minute. I can't just let her disappear. Please."

Victor looked into the crowd. Waved. The masses shifted, parted, shifted again. Finally, Cooper Shaye emerged. Beside him was Jillian.

Shaye stared out through eyes black with pain, dark with a terrible sorrow.

"If I do you this favor, Burke, you must do one for me in return," Cooper Shaye said. "Remember these people. All of them. Not for what you see now, but for what they were. Remember them for the lives they lived, and the people they loved, and the accomplishments they made. You'll do that?"

Jonas nodded.

"One more thing."

"Yes," Jonas said.

"Live your life, as well. Don't shame all of our memories by wasting away, by mourning those who have left. Be happy, Jonas Burke. That is the only way the living can repay what they owe to the dead. Be happy. And laugh in death's face."

Cooper Shaye stepped aside.

Jonas struggled to control the tears that clawed at him, trying to get out. His baby girl stood before him, head bowed. Her hair stringy, skin white, eyes hollow and vacant.

"Jillian. Honey. It's me. Daddy."

She did not move.

"I know you don't remember. I know . . . but I just wanted you to know something . . . something before you go. I want you to know that you were loved. Very much. By your mother. And by me. You were life to us. You were joy. Just know that. Keep it in your heart. Forever."

Jillian turned her head then, cocked it slightly into the cold Chicago night. ". . . you sang to me . . . in bed . . . songs . . ."

Now the tears came. And Jonas Burke did nothing to stop them. "Yes, that's right. I would sing to you. All kinds of songs. When you were happy, when you were sick, when you were tucked in at night."

". . . mother's gonna buy you a diamond ring . . . warm voice . . . happy face . . ."

"Yes."

". . . and you . . . you would push my bike . . . bike . . . I remember that . . . and kiss my forehead sometimes . . . kiss it soft . . . I liked that."

"Yes, I kissed you. You remember."

Jillian then did something Jonas had not expected, something that left him breathless. She turned her head higher. Higher.

And she looked him in the eye. And for a moment they were father and daughter again.

". . . and I remember also . . . I remember that . . . you loved me . . ."

Jonas sobbed. Bit his lip nearly hard enough to draw blood. "Very much. Please carry that with you."

And then she lowered her head again, and Jonas could feel that the beautiful, fleeting moment of recognition he had shared with Jillian was gone. She turned away, lost to him now forever. Withdrawn into her own faraway thoughts. Waiting to find peace.

Jonas sighed. Rubbed his eyes. He felt a strong hand upon his shoulder.

"Cooper's words are wise," Victor said. "I hope you will follow them."

"You'll be by my side, Victor, to make certain that I do."

Victor's shoulders sighed forward. "Jonas, please, don't make this more difficult. You know my intentions."

"Yes, and I know Lucias's intentions, too. He is going to continue, Victor. Every day from here on out, perhaps into eternity. There will be more experiments and more experiments and thousands of others like these poor souls. And at some point there won't be enough fires to consume them all."

"What would you have me do?"

"The same thing I am going to do. Stop him. I won't allow another father to suffer through the torment I have gone through. Come with me, Victor."

Victor peered off into the fire for a moment, the red glare reflected back in his eyes. "I don't know how much longer I can try to mend the mistakes of my past. I am so weary."

"But your life is different now, Victor. You have something you have never had before."

Victor looked away from the fire, back toward Jonas. "And what is that, Jonas Burke?"

Jonas laid a hand upon his shoulder. "A friend."

Victor grinned.

"I'm not altogether certain you know what you are venturing into, Jonas. I have a feeling things will only get worse from here. That Lucias will become even more vicious in his single-minded pursuit."

"Then so will we."

"You believe there is nothing left in this world for you. That Lucias can no longer cause you pain. But, if you go after him, Jonas, take my word. He'll find a way."

The fire had now become a living being, a ravenous, famished beast. The castle groaned under the fury of its attack.

The sirens were only a few blocks away, the night air brittle with their mournful wailing. The trucks would be here in minutes.

"Why didn't you ever do this before?" Jonas said.

Victor squinted. "I do not understand what you are asking."

"If you could end your misery at any time by walking into a fire, why not do it? You've been in pain for two centuries. You could have ended it at any time."

"It is not the fear of dying that torments the minds of men, Jonas. It is the idea of dying *alone*."

It was then that the Hidden began, slowly, to shuffle into the burning house. Slowly. One after the other. There were no screams. Nothing but the sound of the roaring fire.

One of them, skin like chalk, stumbled up to Victor. "Pain will go away, now?" he said.

Victor patted him on the back. Smiled. "Yes, Martin. It will all be better now. You'll see. No more pain."

The man seemed to take comfort in Victor's words. Silently, like a ghost that had been no more than a figment of the imagination, he disappeared into the fire.

Soon, the last of the Hidden had vanished, returned to the earth as dust, their pain erased.

Only two remained on the outskirts of the rumbling flames. Shaye and Jillian.

Shaye looked one more time toward the heavens, toward the ghostly-pale stars, and then he and Jillian turned back toward Jonas, something he had hoped neither would do. Shaye smiled weakly, the first time Jonas could ever recall him doing so. And Jillian, well, perhaps it was just a trick of the light, Jonas thought, or just wish fulfillment, but he could have sworn she smiled back at him too.

Then, holding hands, Shaye and Jonas's daughter walked into the fire.

THE NEXT JOURNEY.

THE MAN CLASPED HIS COLLAR TIGHT, the bitter winter winds tearing at him, raveling his coat, biting at the exposed flesh of his face.

His companion, a large man in a snow-white fur coat, trudged along beside him, hunched slightly, leather gloves covering his mismatched hands.

"He's a man with unlimited resources," the large man said, a series of small scars playing along the perimeters of his face. "He could have laboratories in a hundred different countries. He will not be easy to find. We also have to consider the fact that, one day soon, his experiments may prove successful. That he will resurrect the dead and they will walk alongside man."

"I have a feeling he will not be as hard to locate as you think. I believe there's a part of him that wants to be found."

"And how long do you suppose we'll chase him? How long before this insanity can come to an end?"

The man turned toward his companion, looked into his steel grey eyes. "How much time do you have?"

The large man nudged his friend. Gently. A feeling of kinship toward him he had never before known.

"Forever," the man said.

HOMECOMING.

NO ONE HAD SEEN HIM SCURRY from the rubble.

There had been dozens of survivors, all of them crying, holding their bleeding heads and torn arms and fractured bones. Paramedics did the best they could to tend to their wounds, as news crews swarmed over them like maggots, devouring them for their stories of horror and survival.

But the rescue teams and reporters had not seen him. He had made sure of it. He pulled himself intact from the shattered concrete and twisted metal support rods and splintered glass. For a while he lay in the shadows, beneath an avalanche of cinder blocks. Screaming filled his ears. The clanging of firebells. Shouts of emergency workers.

He had never expected to find her. The odds against it were immense. Beyond reason. And yet, there she was. Stretched out beneath a concrete slab. Crushed. Her body twisted at absurd angles.

He crawled to her, careful not to draw attention to himself. He would have to work quickly. He knew he could not go undetected much longer.

He tugged at her lifeless leg. He could see that the other had been amputated. Cleanly. And her arms . . . both were gone.

She was so beautiful; not even death could change that. He tried to move the concrete, strained his tired muscles against its immense weight; it was no use. He searched the area immediately around him. The shattered detritus of the squalid crack house scattered in all directions.

But nothing that would help him free her.

No, wait, that wasn't true. There was something. Just ahead. A four-inch thick metal support rod, twisted madly but still in one piece. He clambered over the pile of debris, wrenched it free and lodged it tightly beneath the concrete slab. The remains of a metal gurney acted as a fulcrum. He pushed down, splaying his entire weight across the surface of the rod. He could feel it sink beneath him, down, down, and the concrete slab slid free.

He pulled her from the wreckage, and was gone. Right from under their noses.

Now, midnight fast approaching on dark wings, he watched her as she lay on his kitchen table, her leg dangling off the side, her sweet, tender face beginning to blacken and lose its shape.

He had to do something. Soon.

He had learned many things in the dank underbelly of Arch Angel Enterprises. He had seen things no man should ever see. Flesh defiled in ways both unnatural and absurd. Total and arrogant disregard for God's work. An open disdain for the laws of nature.

Yes, he had seen it all. Had watched with his own eyes as bodies were cut apart. And stitched together. Even his own. Even through his screams, he watched as the blade cut through skin, then tendon, then bone.

It was now his obligation to make use of that knowledge. To put what he had learned to work.

So beautiful, he thought, as he watched her. Even with her cheeks showing the first signs of bloating, and her eyes sinking and skin becoming mottled and gray, she was still beautiful. As lovely as anyone he had ever seen.

And he loved her. He realized that now. Maybe for the first time. And he couldn't let death stand in the way.

Walton Wallace walked briskly across the kitchen. With purpose. He pulled open the drawer beside the sink. Inside, metal clanged against metal. He lifted out the largest knife he owned. He had never used it.

He held it to the light, turned it over in his hands, the metal winking. He ran his thumb along the blade. A thin trail of blood seeped out.

Sharp. Very sharp.

He looked back to Judith. Lovely Judith.

He would start with the arms. That would be the easiest.

There was a girl down the hall—Gloria, her name was, or Glenda. She always smiled at Walton when they passed in the hallway. She was pretty and she was about Judith's size. Yes, she would do fine.

He would pay her a visit right now. He was a bit concerned that his knife would have a difficult time chopping through the bone, but he supposed he would find a way. First the arms, then he would take her leg.

He hoped she wouldn't scream too much. He didn't want to see her suffer, but he had to do what must be done.

Then the surgery, as he grafted the limbs to his darling Judith. He could do it. He was sure of it.

And then . . . life. He knew the secret. He had watched it before his very eyes.

Life.

Walton tucked the knife into his waistband at the small of his back. The cold steel felt good against his flesh. It calmed him. Made him realize the wisdom of what he was doing.

He walked down the hallway, toward the girl's apartment.

Smiling.

ACKNOWLEDGEMENTS

Many years ago, after long, late-night writing classes, Mike Martínez, Donna Waters, myself (and any number of other students and faculty from Columbia College Chicago) would sit in the pitch-black windowless morass of the Step Hi Lounge in Chicago's Loop and discuss all the great works of art we would one day unleash upon the world. Those remain some of the finest days of my life, their memory echoing joyously through the corridors of time.

I owe a great debt of thanks to Mr. Martínez for keeping the fire of my youth's passion alive. My hair may be (much) thinner but the joys we discussed in those long-ago days have never waned.

Donna Waters is now Donna Kishbaugh, my wife of several decades. There are not enough hours in the day to tell her how much I love her. How dear she is to me. How much she drives me to do just a little better each day. So I'll tell her here.

Dagan Kishbaugh remains my first and best audience. Each night when he was a child, I would read to him, much of it things I had written just for him. His youthful laughter still rings in my ears, every day. And it never fails to bring a smile.

Bronwyn Kishbaugh is everything I wish I could be. Intellectually inquisitive, morally uncompromised, and determined to work as hard as it takes to meet her every goal. On my darkest days, I turn to her and happily think the world just might have a chance to survive after all.

And I must never forget the ever-shining lights (to name but a few) of Stan Lee and Jack Kirby, Gene Colan and John Romita, Sr., Boris Karloff and Bela Lugosi, and Ray Harryhausen and Ray Bradbury; thanks are due for a million different reasons but especially, in the case of this book, for teaching me that a monster can also have a heart.

ABOUT GREG KISHBAUGH

A Ray Bradbury Fiction Writing Award winner with work appearing in a number of publications including the renowned *Cemetery Dance* magazine, Greg Kishbaugh is the Associate Editor of Evileye Books and the editor of the *Burning Maiden* anthology series. He is the co-founder of Kaleidoscope Entertainment, a company specializing in high-end comics and graphic novels.

ABOUT EVILEYE BOOKS

Evileye Books publishes horror, dark fiction, crime, supernatural thrillers, and science fiction. For more information, please visit our website, Evileyebooks.com.

CPSIA information can be obtained at www.ICGtesting.com
Printed in the USA
LVOW08s1801310114

371835LV00002B/519/P